Chandra Shekhar

Chandra Shekhar

Bankim Chandra Chatterjee

MINT EDITIONS

Chandra Shekhar was first published in 1877.

This edition published by Mint Editions 2021.

ISBN 9781513299396 | E-ISBN 9781513224015

Published by Mint Editions®

 MINT
EDITIONS

minteditionbooks.com

Publishing Director: Jennifer Newens
Design & Production: Rachel Lopez Metzger
Project Manager: Micaela Clark
Translated By: Manmatha Nath Ray Chowdhury
Typesetting: Westchester Publishing Services

Contents

INTRODUCTION

I

The Boy and the Girl

On the bank of the Ganges, there was seated a boy under the green mantles of the mango groves, enjoying the evening melody of the flowing *Bhagirathi*. Under his feet lay, on the green bed of grass, a little girl, casting upon his face her lingering glances—silent and motionless. She was gazing untiringly, and turning for a while her eyes towards the sky overhead, the river below, and the trees around, again fixed them upon that face. The name of the boy was PRATAP—that of the girl, SHAIBALINI. *Shaibalini* was then only a girl of seven or eight—*Pratap* had scarcely stepped into youth.

Overhead, the *Papia*, in its airy flight, filled the sky with waves of music and smoothly glided off. *Shaibalini*, in imitation, began to thrill, with her whistles, the mango groves that adorned the bank of the Ganges. The murmuring melody of the river mingled with that mock music in perfect harmony.

The girl with her little soft hand plucked some equally soft wild flowers, and making with them a garland, embellished the boy with it. Taking it off, she coiled it round her own braid and again put it on the neck of the boy. She could not decide which of them should wear it. At last she got over the difficulty by throwing it round the horns of a plump, nice-looking cow grazing near by. So it happened with them often. Sometimes the boy, in return for the garland, used to bring down for her from the nest of birds their little ones, and in mango season he would give her sweet mangoes ripe for relish.

When the stars appeared in the serene sky of the evening, they began to count them. "Who has seen first?" "Which has first appeared?" "How many do you see?"—"Only four? I see five. There is one, there is another, again there is one, again there is another and lastly mark that." It is a lie. *Shaibalini* does not see more than three.

"Let us count the boats. Can you say how many boats are passing?"— "Only sixteen? Let us bet, I say there are eighteen." *Shaibalini* did not know to count. Once counting she found nine—counting again she came up to twenty-one. Turning from this, they next fixed their eyes upon a particular boat. "Who is in that boat—whence it came—whither it goes? How glittering is the gold in the waters on the oars!"

II

THE DROWNED AND THE RUNAWAY

In this way love's first seed was sown in them. Call it love or give it any other name, it matters not. Only sixteen springs have smiled upon our hero and our heroine is a tiny girl of eight! But no love is so sweet as that which springs from tender hearts.

Early love, it seems, has a curse upon it. How many of those whom you loved in your younger days, you meet in your youth? How many do live to see your youthful days? How many, again, still deserve your love? In old age nothing but the recollection of early love lingers in our memory. But how sweet is that recollection! Every boy, without exception, feels, sometime or other, that yonder girl has an exceptionally sweet face, and that her eyes have some unspeakable charms in them. How often he turns away from his play and looks at her face—how often he lies in wait, in her way, to steal a glance at her. He is never conscious of the feeling, but nevertheless he loves her. Later on, that sweet face and that simple glance are carried away by the current of time—he goes about the world for her, but finds nothing but recollection! Early love, it seems, is cursed.

Shaibalini thought she would be married to *Pratap*. But *Pratap* knew, it was not to be. *Shaibalini* was the daughter of one of *Pratap's* kindreds. The relation was, no doubt, distant, but still they had the same blood in them. This was *Shaibalini's* first mistake.

Shaibalini was a poor man's daughter. She had none but her mother. They had nothing but a cottage and *Shaibalini's* immense beauty. *Pratap* too was very poor.

Shaibalini was growing in years. Her beauty was every day increasing like the new moon, till she reached the height of her glory; but she could not be married. Marriage meant expense, and who would bear it? Who would discover, and pick up, as priceless, that beauty in that wilderness?

Gradually with her years, *Shaibalini* grew wiser. She felt that without *Pratap* there was no happiness in this world. She realised that she had no chance of getting *Pratap* in this life as her husband.

Pratap and *Saibalini* began to consult with each other. They consulted for many days. But none else could know of it, as they did everything in secret. When they came to a decision, they went together for a bath in the Ganges. Many had been swimming in the river then. *Pratap* said, "Come *Shaibalini*, let us swim." They began to swim. Both of them were experts in that art—no one in the village could swim so well as they. It was the rainy season, and the river was full and swollen to the very edge of its banks. Its waters were waving, dancing, and running with mad enthusiasm. They proceeded through that vast sheet of water, tearing its surface, stirring its bosom, and throwing its particles up in the air. In the floating circles of silvery foams, the beautiful young couple looked like a pair of bright jewels set in a silver ring.

When they had gone far away, the people at the *Ghat* shouted and asked them to come back. They would not listen, and proceeded on. Again the people shouted—they called them—they reproached them— they rebuked them, but neither of them would listen—they proceeded on and on. At last they came to a great distance; *Pratap* then cried, "*Shaibalini*, this is our marriage." "No further—let this be the place," responded *Shaibalini* readily, with warmth.

Pratap sank into the water to drown himself. *Shaibalini* did not. Fear came upon her at that moment. She thought within herself, "Why should I die? What is *Pratap* to me? I fear death—my heart fails—I cannot court it." *Shaibalini* turned back, and swam up to the land.

III

A Bridegroom at Last

A boat was passing close to the spot where *Pratap* sank to drown himself. Some one in the boat saw *Pratap* going down, and jumped into the water to his rescue. The man in the boat was *Chandra Shekhar Sharma*.

Chandra Shekhar taking hold of *Pratap*, swam back to the boat, and got him on it. He took his boat to the *Ghat*, landed with *Pratap*, and took him to his house. *Chandra Shekhar* was detained there by *Pratap's* mother. She fell at his feet and prevailed on him to be her guest that day. *Chandra Shekhar*, however, remained ignorant of the secrets of *Pratap's* attempt at suicide.

Shaibalini could not think of appearing before *Pratap* again. But *Chandra Shekhar* saw her and was charmed. *Chandra Shekhar* was not in easy circumstances at the time. He had passed his thirty-second year. He had domestic concerns but had no attraction for this world. He was still a bachelor, and knowing the changes that marriage brings in to be unfavourable to the acquisition of knowledge, he looked upon it with indifference. But lately, a little over a year, his mother had died, and he had already begun to feel that his bachelor life itself was a hinderance. In the first place, he had to cook his food himself, and that took away much of his time—hampered his studies, and his works as a teacher of youths. Secondly, he had a *Shalgram* in his house, whom he worshipped every day. Everything in that connection he had to do himself, and that again, required time. The services of the deity could not be performed without hitches. His household affairs suffered in consequence, yea, it happened sometimes that he could not even get his meals ready. He often missed his books and could not find them out. He often forgot where he kept his money or whom he paid. His income could not cover his expenses, although his wants were very few and small. *Chandra Shekhar* thought his condition would improve, in some respects, if he would marry.

But he resolved that if he would marry at all, he would not marry a beautiful girl; for his mind might become captivated by the charms of a beautiful wife. He would not be entangled in the networks of the world.

When *Chandra Shekhar* was in this mood of mind, he saw *Shaibalini*. The ascetic's determination gave way before her beauty. After much reflection and some hesitation, he at last married *Shaibalini*, himself acting as a match-maker. Who is not captivated by the fascinating influence of beauty?

Our story begins some eight years after this marriage took place.

PART I
THE SINNER

I

DALANI BEGUM

The ruler of Bengal, Behar and Orissa, *Nawab Alija Mir Kasim Khan* was then residing in the *Monghyr* Castle. Within the castle, in the seraglio, was the *Rangamahal*, a part of which was looking exceptionally grand and beautiful. It was still the first part of night. Within the royal apartment, there lay stretched, on the beautifully painted floor, an exceedingly soft piece of carpet. A silver lamp, with fragrant oil, was burning there. The chamber was filled with the fragrance of sweet-scented flowers. Resting her little head on a soft silk pillow, there was lying, on a bed, a young lady of small size and girl-like appearance, reading, with careful study, the difficult texts of the *Gulesthan*. She was seventeen, but her short-built frame made her look like a pretty little girl. She was reading the *Gulesthan*, but at times rose from her study and looked around, muttering within herself a world of things. Sometimes she asked herself, "How is it that he is not yet come?" And the next moment, "Why should he? I am only one of his thousand devoted slaves, why should he come all this distance for me?" She again took to her book. But reading a little, she stopped and said, "I cannot enjoy. Well, he may not come but he can send for me. But why should he think of me at all? I am but one of his thousand devoted slaves." She again began to read the *Gulesthan*, but again closed it, and said, "After all, why God's ways are such? Why does one wait and wait for another, with lingering looks? If that be the will of God, how is it that people do not long for one who is obtainable in life and crave for another who cannot be had? I am a creeper and why do I long to climb the oak?" Then, laying aside the book, she rose up. Her thick curls, which looked like so many flowing snakes, began to swing from her little head, which had a faultless make—the bright golden scarf on her body, which filled the air with sweet fragrance, also began to swing, and a wave of beauty rose in the chamber, as it were, with the very movement of her body, like ripples caused at the slightest agitation in deep waters.

Now, the fair lady took up a little harp, and with a sweet gentle voice began to sing softly, as if she was afraid of listeners. Just then, she heard the greetings of the waiting guards and the footsteps of the *Tanjam* carriers. The girl got startled. She walked up to the entrance in great hurry, and found the *Nawab's Tanjam* there. *Nawab Mir Kasim Ali Khan* alighted from the *Tanjam*, and entered into the chamber. "*Dalani Bibi*, what were you singing just now?" inquired the *Nawab* pleasantly, as he took his seat. The name of the young lady was probably *Doulatunnissa*. The *Nawab* used to call her *Dalani*, perhaps, to abbreviate her name. So, every one in the palace called her *Dalani Bibi* or *Dalani Begum*. *Dalani*, out of bashfulness, remained silent with downcast eyes. To her misfortune the *Nawab* said, "Just sing again what you had been singing. I would like to hear it." Now, everything was upset—the strings of the harp became rebellious—nothing could set them in proper tune. She laid aside the harp and took up a violin. The violin again, it seemed, could not be tuned. The *Nawab* said, "That will do, you just sing with it." At this, *Dalani* came to suspect that the *Nawab* thought she had no good sense of music. Then again, *Dalani* could not open her lips. She attempted several times, but nothing could make them obey her—they remained closed in spite of all efforts. They quivered—they trembled—but, after all, they remained closed. Like the petals of a lily in a cloudy day, they seemed to open but remained closed. Like, a timid poet's verses, or the choked voice of love of a woman, silent in piqued pride, her song seemed to come out but died in her lips.

Then, all on a sudden, *Dalani* laid aside the harp, and said, "I won't sing."

"What is the matter? Are you displeased with me?" inquired the *Nawab* in surprise.

Dalani. I shall never again sing in your presence, unless you get for me one of those musical instruments, which Englishmen, in Calcutta, use when they sing.

"I shall certainly give you one, if nothing stands in the way," said *Mir Kasim* smiling.

Dalani. Why? What would prevent it?

"I am afraid we may fall in a quarrel with the English," observed the *Nawab* in a sad tone, "why, have you not heard of it?"

"Yes, I have," she replied, and then was silent.

Mir Kasim. What are you thinking of so exclusively, *Dalani*?

Dalani. You once told me that any one who would quarrel with the English would surely come to grief—why should you then fight with them yourself? I am a girl, your devoted wife—it is impertinence on my part to speak in a matter like this, but I have a right to say—you are kind to me, you love me.

Mir Kasim. It is true, indeed, I love you, *Dalani*. I never loved nor ever thought of loving a woman so dearly.

Dalani's hairs stood up on their ends. She remained silent for a long time—tears came into her eyes, wiping them away, she said, "If you are sure that whoever would go to fight with the English must be defeated, why are you then preparing for a war against them?" *Mir Kasim*, in a comparatively low voice, replied, "I have no other alternative. I know you are my own, so I say, in your presence, that I know it for certain that in this struggle I shall lose my kingdom, yea, it may be, even my life. Why should I then go for this war at all? Because, the actions of the English go to show that they are the real masters of the country—I am a ruler in name only. What shall I do with that kingdom where I am not the king? Nor is that all. The English say, 'We are the rulers but you shall oppress the people, in our interest.' Why should I do that? If I cannot govern my kingdom for the good of my people, I shall gladly give it up—why should I, for nothing, share in the burden of sin and disgrace? I am neither *Seerajuddaulla* nor *Mirjafar*."

Dalani highly admired in her mind the ruler of Bengal. She said, "My lord, what shall I say to what has fallen from your lips? But I have a favour to ask of you. You must not go to the battle-field yourself."

Mir Kasim. Is it proper that the *Nawab* of Bengal should listen to the counsel of a girl in a matter like this, or is it pertinent for her to thrust her counsel in so serious an affair?

Dalani was put out of countenance—she was mortified, and said, "Excuse me, I have spoken foolishly. A woman has little self-control and that is why I said all these. But I have another prayer."

"What is it?"

"Would you take me to the field along with you?"

"Why? Do you mean to fight yourself? Tell me, I would then dismiss *Gurgan Khan* and appoint you instead.

Dalani was again put to the blush, and this time she could not speak. "Why do you like to accompany me," inquired *Mir Kasim* in an affectionate tone.

"Because I shall be with you," replied *Dalani* suavely, with a charming earnestness.

Mir Kasim declined. Nothing could persuade him to accede to her wishes. *Dalani* then said, with a gentle smile, "My lord! you know to read the future, pray see, where shall I be during the war?"

"Very well, let me have pen and ink," said *Mir Kasim* with a smile.

The attending maid, being asked by *Dalani*, brought in the golden case of pen and ink.

Mir Kasim had learnt astrology from the Hindus. As instructed, he put down some figures, and began to calculate. After a while, he threw away the paper from his hand and became sad. "What is the result of your calculation?" inquired *Dalani* anxiously.

"What I see is very strange. You should not hear it," answered *Mir Kasim* with a melancholy voice.

The Nawab immediately came out, and calling the *Mir Munshi* before him, said, "Issue orders to a Hindu officer, at *Murshidabad*, to send here *Chandra Shekhar*, a learned *Brahmin*, who taught me astrology. He lives at *Bedagram*, a place very close to *Murshidabad*. He should be summoned here to calculate where would *Dalani Begum* be, at the time of, and after, the war with the English, if it breaks out at all."

The *Mir Munshi*, as ordered, sent for *Chandra Shekhar*, at *Murshidabad*.

II

THE BHIMA TANK

On the four sides of the large tank *Bhima*, there were thick rows of palm trees. The golden rays of the setting sun had fallen on the black waters of the tank, and on its dark bosom were painted the dark shadows of the palm trees, with the sun-shine between them. By the side of a *ghat*, a small group of shrubby plants, closely knitted together by clustering creepers, served to screen the bashful beauties, playing merry pranks in the water, with their out-stretched boughs. Under the covered shade of that grove, *Shaibalini* and *Sundari*, with brass pails in their hands, were in frolic and play with the water.

What does a play between water and a young woman mean? We do not understand it. He, whose heart beauty has melted into water, can alone say what it is. He alone can say how water, being stirred by the pail, breaks into ripples and dances, in perfect harmony, with the melodious music of the ringing ornaments in a woman's hands. He alone can say how it, embellishing her bosom with a garland of its bubbles, dances in that musical concord. He alone can say how it, rocking the playful swimming little bird on its surface, dances in accompaniment to that ringing music. He alone can say how it, raising its little curling waves, leaps and frisks about her hands, her neck, her shoulders and breast, well-regulated by that melodious tune—again, how the sportive beauty in her turn, floating her pail on the surface of the water, entrusting it to the care of the gentle breeze, dips herself in the water up to the chin, touches it with her purple lips, takes it within her little mouth, and sends it up in the air towards the sun—the water while falling down presents her with a hundred sun, in all its glittering particles. At the very movement of her limbs the water dances and shoots up in silvery fountains. Her heart at the same time dances with the waving ripples of the water. Both are of the same nature! Water is fickle and so also the all-captivating heart of women. Water takes no impression, does a young woman's heart take?

The golden rays of the evening sun gradually faded away in the black waters of the tank, and in a moment everything became dark. Only the top of the palm trees began to scintillate like golden flags.

Sundari cried out, "Well, it is getting late. We should not be here any longer. Let us go home."

Shaibalini. No one is here to listen to us, just softly sing a song, dear.

Sundari. Stop, thou naughty creature; come home.

Shaibalini then playfully uttered the first few lines of a Bengali love song—

> *"To home I won't return,*
> *My love, look, here he comes;*
> *To home I won't return."*

Sundari. What a curse it is! Your love is at home, better go there.

Shaibalini. Go and tell him that his sweet-love, finding the waters of the *Bhima* delightfully cool, has drowned herself in it.

Sundari. Enough, keep your joke aside. It is getting late, I can't wait any longer. Besides, *Khemi's* mother was telling us that a whiteman has come in our village!

Shaibalini. What need you and I fear in that?

Sundari. Oh, you surprise me! get up or I am off.

Shaibalini. I won't, you better go.

Sundari, in anger, filled her pail and got up on the bank. Turning towards *Shaibalini*, she again said, "I say, do you really mean to keep here alone, at this late hour?" *Shaibalini* did not answer, she only pointed out something with her finger. *Sundari* turned her eyes in that direction—on the other side of the tank, under a palm tree, oh, horrible! *Sundari*, without uttering a single word, threw down her pail and ran away breathless. The brass pail rolled down the slope, vomiting forth the water within it with a gurgling sound, and entered into the waters of the tank. *Sundari* had seen a whiteman under the palm tree.

Shaibalini, however, stood firm—she did not get up—she only dipped herself into the water up to her breast, and covering with the wet cloth her braid and only a portion of her head, she remained there like a smiling lily floating on water. A constant flash of lightning smiled in the dark clouds—a golden lily bloomed in the dark ripples of the *Bhima*.

The Englishman now finding *Shaibalini* alone, stealthily came up very close to the *ghat*

" . . . she remained there like a smiling lily. . ."

under the cover of the palm trees. The man was indeed young by appearance. He did not wear a beard or a moustache. His hairs were rather black and his eyes rather dark for an Englishman. He was very gaudily dressed, and there was indeed a good exhibition of chain, ring and other like decorations.

He slowly came up to the *ghat*, and drawing near the water, said, "I come again, fair lady."

Shaibalini. I don't understand your jargon.

Foster. Oh-ay that nasty gibberish—I must speak it, I suppose. *Ham again ayahaya* (I come again).

Shaibalini. Why? Is this the way to *Yama's* gate?

The Englishman failing to understand her asked, "*Keya bolta haya?*" (What do you say, lady?)

Shaibalini. I say, has *Yama* forgotten you?

Foster. *Yama*! *John* you mean? I am not *John*, I am *Lawrence*.

Shaibalini. It is good after all, I have learnt an English word.— *Lawrence* means monkey.

In that late hour of the evening, *Lawrence Foster* thus ridiculed by *Shaibalini* returned to his own place.

Descending the mounds of the tank, *Lawrence Foster* untied his horse from the mango tree and rode away, singing lowly the song, he once heard with its echoes from the resounding hills on the banks of the Teviot. At times, he spoke within himself, "The fascination of the snow-white *Mary Foster*, in which I lost myself in my younger days, is now but a dream. Does change come in the taste of a man, when he comes to live in another land? Is the snow-white *Mary* to be favourably compared with the flaming beauty of the tropics? I cannot decide."

When *Foster* left, *Shaibalini* gently filled her pail and with it she slowly returned home, like the gliding clouds on the back of the gentle breeze of spring. Putting the pail in the proper place, she entered into the bedroom.

In that room, *Shaibalini's* husband, *Chandra Shekhar*, sitting on a small piece of blanket stretched on the floor, and having tied, for close attention, both of his thighs with the waist, by a rag painted with sacred symbols, was reading old manuscripts, in the light of the earthen lamp before him. A hundred years have passed since the time of which we are speaking. *Chandra Shekhar* was then about forty years of age. He was tall in stature, and his body was proportionately stout. He had a large head, with a broad forehead, which was anointed with *Chandan*.

While entering the bedroom, *Shaibalini* thought what she would say to her husband when he would inquire the cause of her returning so late. *Chandra Shekhar*, however, did not say a word when she entered into the room. He was then busily engaged in making out the sense of a particular text of the *Brahmasutras*.

Now, *Shaibalini* burst into laughter. It was then that *Chandra Shekhar* looked up, and asked, "Why is the flash of beauty so untimely today?"

Shaibalini. I thought you would chide me in anger.

Chandra Shekhar. Why?

Shaibalini. Because I am late in returning from the *ghat*.

Chandra Shekhar. Oh, I see! You are just come! Why so late?

Shaibalini. An Englishman had come to the *ghat*. Your cousin *Sundari* was on the bank at the time and she ran away leaving me alone. I was in the water and could not come up for fear. I went further down and stood motionless where the water reached my neck. I could not get up and come home till the man had left."

"Don't come again," he said in abstraction and again fixed his mind on *Shankar's* Commentary.

Night advanced far. Even then, *Chandra Shekhar* was absorbed in the discussion of *Prama*, *Maya*, *Sphota* and *Apaurusheyatya*. *Shaibalini* was sleeping soundly on a bed, in one corner of the room, after she had kept, as usual, her husband's dishes close by him and had taken her own meals. She had *Chandra Shekhar's* permission to do so every day; for he used to study far in the night and could not take his meals early and retire.

All on a sudden, the hoarse voice of an owl came from the roof of the house. *Chandra Shekhar* perceiving that the night had far advanced closed his book and putting it in the proper place, stood up to shake off his drowsiness. His eyes fell upon the beauty of nature which smiled in the moonlight, beyond the open window of his room. The radiant beams of the moon had fallen on the beautiful face of the sleeping *Shaibalini*. *Chandra Shekhar* with a delightful heart saw that smiling face and thought, a lily had bloomed on the waters of a pond, in the radiance of the glorious moon. Standing there motionless, he gazed untiringly—his eyes beaming with joy—at *Shaibalini's* faultless face. Under her dark brows, which were as beautiful as a pair of most artistically painted bows, he saw her beautiful closed eyes, resembling two lilies with folded petals. He saw beautiful fine lines on her thin eyelids, as are seen on the leaf of a tree. He saw that her soft little palm was placed upon her cheek in the unconsciousness of sleep—it appeared, as if, some one had scattered flowers upon flowers.

Her beautiful set of pearl-like teeth could be slightly seen between her sweet rosy lips, which had parted a little under the pressure of the hand over her cheek. The sleeping *Shaibalini* smiled, perhaps, in a pleasant dream—it appeared, as if, there was a flash in the silvery sky of a moonlit night. Her face again became placid in deep slumber. The serene but smiling face of that young lady of twenty, which did not seem to be ruffled by passion, brought tears in *Chandra Shekhar's* eyes. He thought within himself, "Alas! why have I married *Shaibalini*? This jewel would adorn the crown of a king—why have I brought it in the cottage of a poor *Brahmin*, who is always busy with his books? No doubt, she has brought to me happiness with her, but what is that to *Shaibalini*? My age renders it impossible for her to love me—nor can my love quench the thirst of her yearning heart. Particularly, I am always busy with my books and when do I care for *Shaibalini's* happiness? What pleasure so young a lady can have in taking care of my books? I selfishly looked to my own happiness and that is why I could think of marrying her. What shall I do now? Shall I throw into water all the books, which I have collected with great pains and make the lily-like face of a woman as my life's sole object of adoration? Oh shame! I cannot do that. Will then poor *Shaibalini* undergo a penance for my sins? Ah me, did I pluck this beautiful flower, from its stalk, only to see it wither in the fire of unsatiated passions?"

Chandra Shekhar in his abstraction forgot to take his meals. Next morning, a message came from the *Mir Munshi* that *Chandra Shekhar* was to start for *Murshidabad*—the *Nawab* had some business with him.

III

Lawrence Foster

The East India Company had a silk factory at *Purandarpur*, a village very close to *Bedagram*. *Lawrence Foster* was in charge of that factory. When young, *Lawrence* was disappointed in his love for *Mary Foster* and came to Bengal as a servant of the East India Company. As Englishmen now-a-days become affected with various diseases when they come to India, so, in former times the Indian atmosphere used to disease their mind with a lust for plunder. After his arrival in India, *Foster* soon fell a victim to this evil influence. *Mary's* image, therefore, disappeared from his mind's eye. Once he had been to *Bedagram* on some business—his eyes fell upon the smiling lily-like *Shaibalini*, in the waters of the *Bhima*. *Shaibalini* ran away at the sight of a whiteman, but *Foster* returned to the factory reflecting all the way. Thinking on and on, he at last decided that dark eyes were prettier than pale-blue eyes and black hairs were finer than brown ones. All on a sudden, the idea crossed his mind that in the troubled sea of the world, woman is, as it were, a raft and that every man should seek her help. Those Englishmen are indeed very clever, who take Bengalee beauties as companions of their life and thus save the clergyman's dues. Many Bengalee girls have been seduced to worship English profligates for money—may not *Shaibalini* be tempted to do so? *Foster*, accompanied by a native officer of the factory, came to *Bedagram* again and both of them remained concealed in a bush. The officer saw *Shaibalini* and marked out her house.

Bengalee children, as a class, get frightened at the very mention of a bugbear but there are such naughty children too as would like to see it. So it happened with *Shaibalini*. At first she, as usual in those days, used to run away breathless whenever she met *Foster*. Afterwards some one told her, "The Englishman does not swallow a man alive—he is a curious animal—just look, at him once." *Shaibalini* did so—she found that the Englishman really did not swallow her alive. Since then *Shaibalini* never ran away at the sight of *Foster* and gradually grew bold enough to speak with him. This is known to our readers.

In an inauspicious moment *Shaibalini* came into this world and in an inauspicious moment *Chandra Shekhar* accepted her hand. We shall gradually say what *Shaibalini* was, but however that may be, *Foster's* attempts did not succeed.

Later on, *Foster* unexpectedly received an order from Calcutta, that as another man had been appointed for the factory at *Purandarpur*, he was to leave for *Calcutta* immediately—he would be deputed on a special duty. The man who was to relieve him, came along with the order. *Foster*, therefore, had to start for *Calcutta* forthwith.

Shaibalini's beauty had completely captivated *Foster's* mind. He could feel that he was to leave the place giving up the hope of getting *Shaibalini* in this life. In those days, the Englishmen who came to live in Bengal were incapable of two things only—they would never plead inability and could never overcome temptations. They could under no circumstance make up their mind to say that they had failed to do a thing and so they must desist from it, and they would never admit that a certain thing was wrong and should not, therefore, be undertaken at all. In this world, there was, perhaps, never seen a class of men more powerful, and self-indulgent than those who laid the foundation of British rule in India. *Lawrence Foster* was a man of that type. He did not restrain his lust—in those days the word *religion* was extinct among Englishmen in Bengal. *Foster* did not even think of consequences—he said within himself, "Now or never"—and made for *Bedagram* with a *palanquin*, some porters and a few servants of the factory, fully armed, on the night previous to the day he was to start for *Calcutta*. On that very night, the inhabitants of *Bedagram* heard with fear that *Chandra Skekhar's* house was being looted by *Dacoits*. *Chandra Shekhar* was not at home. He had gone to *Murshidabad* and had not yet returned. The villagers hearing the noise, the shrieks and the reports of guns left their bed, came out and saw that *Chandra Shekhar's* house was being plundered—there were many torch-lights. No body came forward to the rescue. They saw, from a distance, that the *Dacoits*, after plundering the house, came out one by one; they also saw, in astonishment, that some porters came out of the house with a *palanquin* on their shoulders. Its shutters were closed—the *Sahib* of the *Purandarpur* factory was himself following it very closely. At this sight, every one turned aside quietly, in fear.

When the plunderers had left, *Chandra Shekhar's* neighbours entered into his house and found that very few articles had been taken away. But, *Shaibalini* was not there! Some said, "She must have hid herself somewhere and will soon return." The old men, however, said, "She will never return—even if she does, *Chandra Shekhar* will not take her in.

She must have gone in the *palanquin* we have seen." Those who expected that *Shaibalini* would soon return, waited and waited for her till they grew tired and sat down. Sitting there for a long time, they began to doze, and at last left the place in disgust. *Sundari*, the young lady whom we have already introduced, left last of all. She was the daughter of one of *Chandra Shekhar's* neighbours. She stood in the relation of a cousin to him, and was *Shaibalini's* constant companion. We shall have occasion to speak of her hereafter, and hence this introduction.

Sundari waited for *Shaibalini* the whole night. She returned home in the morning and began to weep.

IV

The Barber Woman

*F*oster himself escorted the *palanquin* up to the bank of the *Bhagirathi*. A large boat, comfortable for ladies to live in, was kept there in readiness. *Shaibalini* was taken up on that boat. *Foster* engaged *Hindu* servants for her and some sentries to keep watch. What was the necessity for *Hindu* servants now?

Foster proceeded to *Calcutta* in another boat. He was to travel fast; it would be quite impossible for him to reach *Calcutta* in a week's time, if he was to go in *Shaibalini's* big boat, making its way against the wind. He did so, because he had no such fear that in his absence some one might attack the boat and rescue *Shaibalini*. He thought that none would dare to approach the boat for the simple fact that it belonged to an Englishman. He left instructions that *Shaibalini's* boat should be taken to *Monghyr*.

Shaibalini's spacious boat, mounting upon the chain of little waves raised by the morning breeze, was moving towards the north. The murmuring ripples were breaking under the boat with a pattering noise. You can trust a rogue, a cheat or an imposter, but not the morning breeze. The gentle breeze of the morning is very delightful—it steals in like a thief and softly plays here with a lily, there with a bunch of jessamine and elsewhere with a branch of the fragrant *Bakul*. It brings sweet fragrance to some—takes away other's dullness after sleep—it soothes the troubled head of another, and when it finds a young beauty it gives a gentle puff at her locks and slips away. Suppose you are in a boat—you see the gentle sportive morning breeze beautifully adorning the river with garlands of ripples—removing the thin isolated clouds in the sky and making it clear and serene; again, you find it gently waving the trees on the banks, playing merry pranks with young beauties bathing in the river, and coming under your boat making a delightful music for your ears. You at once think that air is by nature very gentle, very sober and absolutely free from boisterous tumult, yet ever cheerful and gay! Oh, what good would not have been possible, if everything in this world had been so! You at once cry out, "No fear, start the boat." Then, the sun gradually appears above the horizon—you see its rays glittering on the curling waves of the river; they have now become a little bigger—the swans are waving on them, as if they were dancing; the earthen pails of the beauties, busily engaged in washing themselves, cannot rest on them—they are capering about briskly; sometimes, the waves with unwarrantable intrepidity take liberties with the fair ones and leap upon their shoulders; again, they throw themselves at the feet of her who has got ashore—strike their heads against them in expectation of favour, as if saying, "Oh, be pleased to give us shelter in thy feet." At any rate, they lightly wash away the red paint from her feet and tint themselves with it, in pride and pleasure. Later on, you notice that the sound of the wind is gradually increasing—it no more faints away in the ear like *Joydev's* sweet and delicate verses—it no more plays on the harp the soft melodious *Bhairaby*. At last, you find that the wind has become uproarious in its noise—the air is filled with tumultuous howls; the waves have suddenly got swollen, and rocking their proud heads, break in dashing fury; a gloom is cast all around; a head-wind stands in the way of your boat and getting hold of its prow, strikes it against the water—at times, it turns the face of the boat backwards—you understand what all these mean, and making a nod to the God of wind for your experience, take your boat to the shore!

The same thing happened with *Shaibalini's* boat. Not long after dawn, the wind became very strong. The big boat could not proceed any farther against the head-wind. The men escorting *Shaibalini*, took it to the *Ghat*, at *Vadrahati*.

A barber woman came near the boat a little after its arrival there. She had her husband alive and was, therefore, clothed in a *Shari* with red borders—it had also red figure-works at the corner ends. She had in her hand a small basket, containing *Alta*. The woman, seeing the black-bearded men on the boat, drew the veil over her face. They were looking at her in dumb surprise.

Shaibalini's food was being cooked on a *Char*, near by. *Hindu* practices were still being observed. A *Brahmin* was cooking for her. One cannot get anglicised in a day! *Foster* knew, that if *Shaibalini* would not slip out of his hands, or commit suicide, she would surely one day sit at a dinner-table and take English dishes with relish. He thought, he should not be impatient; for, impatience would certainly mar all prospects. Considering all these, *Foster*, as advised by his servants, had engaged a *Brahmin* cook to accompany *Shaibalini*. The *Brahmin* was cooking and a maid-servant was there to assist him. The barber woman came to that maid-servant and said, "Where do you come from, please?" The maid-servant got out of her temper—no wonder, as she drew her pay from an Englishman—and said, "We come from *Hilly—Delhi—Mecca*, what does it matter to you, wretched woman?" She felt awkward at this and said, "Well, I don't mean anything wrong. I am a barber woman—I am only enquiring if my services be required by any lady in your boat." The maid-servant was pacified a little and said, "All right, let me enquire." She then went to *Shaibalini* to ask her if she would have her feet painted with *Alta*. No matter for what reason, *Shaibalini* was seeking for a diversion, and she said, "Yes, I will." The maid-servant then sent the barber woman within the boat, with the permission of the guards. She herself remained engaged in the cookery, as before.

The barber woman drew down her veil a little more when she saw *Shaibalini*. She then placed one of *Shaibalini's* feet on her hand and began to paint it. *Shaibalini* gazed at the woman very attentively for sometime. She then said,

"Barber woman, where do you live?"

Shaibalini got no answer—she again asked,

"What's your name?"

Yet she got no reply.

"Are you weeping?"

"No," softly replied the woman, this time.

"Yes, you are," said *Shaibalini* and removed the woman's veil. She was really weeping but she smiled a little when the veil was taken off.

"I made you out as soon as you stepped in," said *Shaibalini* smiling. "You cover your face with a veil before me—what a curse it is! Now, where do you come from?"

The barber woman was no other than *Sundari* herself. Wiping away her tears, *Sundari* said, "Hasten off—put on my *Shari*—I will change it for yours. Take this little basket in your hand and go away from the boat, drawing a veil over your face."

"How could you manage to come here?" inquired *Shaibalini*, in abstraction.

Sundari. Whence I came and how I came, I will explain to you hereafter, if I live to see a better day. I have come here in search of you. People said, that the *palanquin* had gone towards the *Ganges*. So, leaving my bed early in the morning, I walked up to the bank of the *Ganges*, without giving out my mind to any one. People there said, that the *Budgerow* had gone towards the north. It is a long way from home and my legs became weak with pain. I then hired a boat and followed you up to this place. Your boat is big—it hardly moves—mine was a small one, and so I have overtaken you so soon.

Shaibalini. How could you come alone?

It came to *Sundari's* lips, "How could you, you shameless wretch, come away in the *palanquin* of a *Sahib*?" But she controlled her tongue, thinking that it was not the proper time for such a reproach. She said, "I have not come alone. My husband is with me. I have come here in the disguise of a barber woman, keeping our little boat at a distance."

"Then, what next?" carelessly inquired the absent-minded *Shaibalini.*

Sundari. Now, put on my *Shari*, take this little basket of *Alta* in your hand and go down from the boat, veiling your face—no one will be able to detect you. You are to go along the bank. You will find my husband waiting in a small boat. Don't feel any delicacy before him—get on the boat at once and take your seat there. He will set out, the very moment you will get on the boat and take you home.

Shaibalini meditated for a long time, and then said, "But, what will be your fate?"

Sundari. Don't be anxious for me. No such Englishman has yet come to Bengal as can cabin *Sundari* in a boat. I am a *Brahmin's* daughter and a *Brahmin's* wife; in this world we have no danger to dread, if we are pure and firm within ourselves. You go, anyhow I will come home by tonight. I believe in God, the saviour in distress. Don't delay any more—my husband has not yet taken his meals—God knows, whether he will have any today.

Shaibalini. Well, suppose I go home, would my husband take me back?

Sundari. Oh, nonsense! Why should he not? It is no joke.

Shaibalini. Just see, an Englishman has snatched me away from my home—ah me, I have lost my caste in the eyes of the world!

Sundari looked at *Shaibalini's* face in surprise, and began to scan it very closely. She cast her acute penetrating glances upon her—like a charmed snake, proud *Shaibalini* lowered her head. *Sundari* then asked, in a rather stern manner, "Will you tell me the truth?"

Shaibalini. Yes, I will.

Sundari. Here, on the sacred waters of the *Ganges*?

Shaibalini. Yes, I will. You need not ask me; I will, of my own accord, tell you what you want to know of me. I have not yet come in contact with the *Sahib*—my husband will not fall from grace, if he will take me back.

Sundari. If that be so, do not doubt that your husband will receive you back. He is pious and will not do you injustice; so, don't waste time in idle talks.

Shaibalini remained silent for a time. She wept a little, and then wiping away her tears, said, "I may go, my husband may also take me in—but, will my stain be ever removed?"

Sundari made no reply. *Shaibalini* continued, "Hereafter, will not the little girls of our village point me out with their fingers and cry out, 'Look, that woman was taken away by an Englishman'? God forbid it, if I ever have a son, who will dine in my house when invited at his *Annaprasan* ceremony? If I ever get a daughter, what *Brahmin* of high lineage will marry his son with her? If I go back now, who will believe that I have not lost my caste? How shall I again appear before society?"

Sundari. You have been fated to this condition and now there is no help for it. Throughout your life, you shall have to endure a little humiliation; but, still you shall be in your own home.

Shaibalini. For what pleasure? In the hope of what enjoyment should I return home to endure so much pain? No father, no mother, no friend—

Sundari. Why, have you not a husband? For whom else is the life of a woman?

Shaibalini. You know everything—

Sundari. Yes, I know. I know that you are the greatest sinner amongst the sinners of this world. Your heart is not contented with the love of a husband, the like of whom is very rare on earth. His only fault is that he does not know how to caress his wife in the very same way as a boy fondles his doll in the play-room. He is again to blame, because, God has not made him a motley clown but a true man. He is pious and learned, whereas you are a sinner; why should you be contented with him? You are worse than blind and that is why you cannot see that the love which your husband bears to you is such as is rarely enjoyed by a woman. It was your good luck and the result of your past deeds of piety that you received so much affection from so good a husband. However that may be, no more of this—it is not the time for such a talk. Even if he does not love you, still, if you can pass your days in worshipping him, your life's highest aim will be attained. Why are you making further delay? I am getting annoyed.

Shaibalini. You see, when I was at home, I used to think that if I could find a relative on my father's or mother's side, I Would go and live with him, or else I would go to *Benares* and live there on alms, or I would drown myself in water. Now I am going to *Monghyr*. Let me go there and see how I like the place. Let me see whether I can get alms in that city. If I am to put an end to my life, I will do that. Death is at my will. What other alternative have I now but to die? But, whether I live or die, I have resolved not to return home. You have, for nothing, taken so much trouble—go back, I will not return. Think me dead. Be sure, sooner or later, I will die. You better go home.

After this, *Sundari* made no further request. Checking her tears, she rose up and said, "I trust, you will soon die. I earnestly pray to God that you may have sufficient courage to court death. May your life come to an end before you reach *Monghyr*. May death come upon you either through storm, or tempest, or the capsize of your boat, before you get into that city." *Sundari* then came out of the boat. She threw into the water the basket of *Alta* and returned to her husband.

V

CHANDRA SHEKHAR'S RETURN

Chandra Shekhar read the future, with the help of Astrology. He then said to the state-officer, "Please report to the *Nawab* that I have failed to calculate."

"Why, sir?" inquired the officer in surprise.

"Everything cannot be ascertained by astrological calculations", replied *Chandra Shekhar*. "If that was possible, man would have been omniscient. Besides, I am not an expert in Astrology."

"Is it so, or a prudent man does not give out a thing, unpleasant to the king?" observed the officer shrewdly. "However that may be, I shall report to the *Nawab* just what you have said."

Chandra Shekhar left for home. The *Nawab's* officer did not dare to offer him his travelling expenses. *Chandra Shekhar* was both a *Brahmin* and a *Pandit* but not a *Brahmin-Pandit*, as the saying goes. He would never accept any offer of money.

While returning home, *Chandra Shekhar* saw his house from a distance. The moment he saw it, his heart was filled with joy.

Chandra Shekhar was a metaphysician, and he was naturally very inquisitive. He said within himself, "How is it that while returning from a distant country, one's heart leaps up with joy at the very sight of his home? Did I in any way suffer, these days, for food and rest? When I shall reach home, what will make me happier there than what I have been while abroad? No doubt, at this advanced age, I have fallen into the inextricable snare of this world. My dear wife lives in that yonder house. Does that account for my joy? In this universe everything has emanated from the same God. If that be so, why do we love some and despise others? Every one has come from the same universal stock! How is it that I do not at all wish to look back at the man who is following me with my bundle, but eagerly desire to behold the smiling lily-like face of that fair one? I do not disregard the commandments of God, but I feel I am getting entangled in the intricate net-work of this World. Then again, I never wish to come out of the snare—if I live through eternity, I shall eagerly desire to remain buried in the illusion of this charm through endless time. O, When shall I see *Shaibalini* again!"

All on a sudden, a fear came into *Chandra Shekhar's* mind. He thought, "If on my return I do not find *Shaibalini*! Why should I not? If she is ill! every one gets ill some time or other—she will be all right again. Why do I feel so uneasy at the very thought of her illness? Who does not get ill at times? If *Shaibalini* has been attacked with a serious illness!" *Chandra Shekhar* began to walk faster. He again thought, "If *Shaibalini* is ill, God will bring her round—I will propitiate the stars with the help of the *sastras*. If she does not recover!" Tears came into *Chandra Shekhar's* eyes. He asked within himself, "Will God deprive me of the jewel, he has been pleased to give me at this advanced stage of my life? It may not be impossible—am I so much in His grace that He will confer upon me weal only and never woe? It might be that some great misery is in store for me. If on my return home, I see that *Shaibalini* is not there—if I hear that *Shaibalini* has succumbed to a serious illness! Oh, that will kill me." *Chandra Shekhar* now began to walk still faster. Reaching the village, he marked that his neighbours were looking at his face very gravely—he could not understand what those looks meant. The boys laughed in their sleeves at the very sight of him—some followed him from at a distance. The old men of the village turned their backs, as they saw him coming. All these astonished *Chandra Shekhar*—frightened him and made *Shaibalini* the sole object of his thought. He looked to no side and came up straight to the gate of his house. The doors were closed. The servant opened the entrance of the outer apartment of the house when it was knocked from outside. He burst into a scream when he saw *Chandra Shekhar*. *Chandra Shekhar* anxiously enquired, "What is the matter?" The servant gave no answer and left the place, crying loudly as he passed. *Chandra Shekhar* took the name of the God of his adoration. He saw that the courtyard had not been cleansed for a long time—there were filth and dirt in the sacred apartments of the household Gods. Here and there, he saw burnt torches and broken doors. *Chandra Shekhar* entered into the female quarters and found that the doors of all the rooms were closed from without. He noticed that the maid-servant walked out in silence when she saw him, and began to cry aloud from outside. After this, *Chandra Shekhar*, standing in the courtyard, called out in a shrill unnatural voice,

"*Shaibalini*!"

No one responded to the call. So unnatural was *Chandra Shekhar's* voice that even the weeping maid-servant became quiet in painful surprise.

Chandra Shekhar cried out again. His voice resounded in the house, but no one responded.

By that time the red ensign of the English on *Shaibalini's* green boat was waving in the gentle breeze of the Ganges—the boatmen were singing in chorus.

******

Chandra Shekhar came to know every thing. He then removed from his house the idol *Shalgram*, which he had installed there with great devotion, as his household God, and placed it at *Sundari's* father's house. He next called in his poor neighbours and distributed among them his clothes, utensils, and other household articles. In the evening he gathered together the books, he had read and was to read, and which were to him as dear as his life-blood. He next brought them all in the courtyard one by one, and while doing so, he occasionally opened this or that book, but closed every one of them without reading a line. When all the books were arranged in a heap, he set fire to it.

The fire blazed forth. It gradually touched mythology, history, poetry, rhetoric, and grammar. Laws and codes of *Manu, Jajnavalka* and *Parasar*, philosophy of the schools of *Nyaya, Vedanta, Shankhya* and others, *Kalpasutra, Arannyak* and *Upanishad*, all took fire one by one. The priceless treasure of old books, which had been collected with great pains, became reduced to ashes. The books were all burnt down by the first part of the night, when *Chandra Shekhar* left his house with only a simple sheet on his body. Whither he left for, no one came to know and no one enquired about it.

PART II
THE SIN

I

KULSAM

No, the bird won't dance. Now tell your story, said *Dalani Begum*, and pulled the peacock that did not dance by its tail-coverts. She then took off from her hand the diamond bracelet, and put it round the neck of another peacock. She next squirted the face of a parrot with rose-water. The parrot chidingly cried out, "slave." *Dalani* herself had taught the bird this word of reproach.

Close by, a maid-servant was trying to make the birds dance. To her *Dalani* had said, "Now, tell your story."

Kulsam said, "It is nothing more than this. Two boats loaded with arms have arrived at the *Ghat*. An Englishman is in charge of them; those two boats have been seized by our men. *Ali Ibrahim Khan* is of opinion that the boats should be allowed to pass. If they are detained under arrest, a quarrel with the English will unnecessarily arise. But *Gurgan Khan* says that let a quarrel arise if it will—the boats must not be let off."

Dalani. To what place are the arms being sent?

Kulsam. To the factory at *Azimabad*. If war be inevitable, it shall first break out there. The English are sending arms there so that they may not be dislodged from that place all on a sudden. This is the rumour in the castle.

Dalani. But why does *Gurgan Khan* want to keep the boats under arrest?

Kulsam. He says that it will be very difficult to win the battle if the enemies. are allowed to grow in strength. *Ali Ibrahim Khan*, however, thinks that whatever we may do, we shall never be able to defeat the English in a fight—so we must not quarrel with them. Why should we then provoke a battle by arresting the boats? In fact, his words are very true. There is no escaping out of the hands of the English. I fear, the scene of what happened to *Seerajuddaulla* is going to be re-enacted.

Dalani remained absorbed in meditation for a long time. At last she said, "*Kulsam*, can you make bold to perform a daring deed?"

Kulsam. What's it? Am I to eat a *Hilsa* fish or take a bath in cold water?

Dalani. Stop, thou naughty fool. It is no joke. If the *Nawab* comes to know of it, he will throw both of us under the feet of an elephant.

Kulsam. But can he know of it at all? I have stolen much essence and scented water, gold and silver, but just say, who has come to know of it? It seems to me that in the case of men, the two eyes are given only to beautify the head—they don't see anything with them. I don't remember to have ever seen a man detecting the trickery of a woman.

Dalani. Fool! I don't mean the eunoch attendants. The *Nawab* is certainly not like ordinary men. What can he not know and understand?

Kulsam. What can I not hide and conceal? Now, what am I to do?

Dalani. Only a letter shall have to be sent to the Commander-in-chief.

Kulsam remained silent in surprise. *Dalani* asked, "What do you say to this?"

Kulsam. Who will address the letter?

Dalani. I myself.

Kulsam. How is it? Have you run mad?

Dalani. Almost.

For a time both of them remained seated in silence. Finding them so, the two peacocks got up, each on their own resting rod, and the parrot began to cry aloud in vain. The other birds turned their attention to their foods.

A little after *Kulsam* said, "The task is light—if a eunoch attendant be given something he will forthwith carry the letter to the proper quarter. But it is at the same time very difficult—if the *Nawab* comes to know of it, both of us shall be put to death. However that may be, it is your business and you understand it better—I am your servant and I must obey you. Let me have the letter and something in cash.

Kulsam left with the letter. This letter formed the thread by which God knitted together the fates of *Dalani* and *Shaibalini*.

II

Gurgan Khan

The name of the person to whom *Dalani's* letter was carried, was *Gurgan Khan*. *Gurgan Khan* was the highest and the ablest of all the officers of the *Nawab*, in Bengal, at the time. He was an Armenian by nationality. *Ispahan* was his birth place. Rumour has it that he was originally a cloth-dealer. But he was a man of uncommon parts and abilities. Within the short period of his service under the *Nawab*, he obtained the exalted post of the Commander-in-chief. Nor was that all; after his appointment as the Commander-in-chief, he organised a rifle-corps and trained and armed it after the European fashion. The guns and rifles which he got made in Bengal under his supervision, surpassed in quality even those made in Europe. His rifle-corps in every respect became equal to that of the English. *Mir Kasim* had hoped so far that with *Gurgan Khan's* help he would overthrow the English. *Gurgan Khan's* influence consequently became very great. *Mir Kasim* would do nothing without consulting him. The *Nawab* would never listen to anything said against his advice. So *Gurgan Khan* had virtually become a bit of a *Nawab*. The Mahamedan high officials, therefore, got annoyed.

It was midnight, yet *Gurgan Khan* had not retired to bed. Alone in the room, he was reading some letters, in the light of a lamp. They were addressed to him by some Armenians from *Calcutta*. After reading the letters, *Gurgan Khan* called out his attendant. The waiter came in and stood before him to receive orders.

"Are all the doors open?" Inquired *Gurgan Khan*.

"Yes, if it please you," replied the attendant.

Gurgan Khan. Have you made it known to all that if any one comes to me at this hour, nobody should stop that visitor or enquire the person's name?

"Yes sir, your order has been carried out," replied the man.

Gurgan Khan. All right, you now keep away.

Gurgan Khan then bundled up the letters, and concealed them in a safe place. He then said within himself, "Now, what course should I follow? India is now an ocean, so to speak—one would pick up as many gems as often he would dive into it. What gain will there be if I simply count the waves from the shore? Well, I used to sell cloth measuring it out with the yard, but now India is afraid of me; I am the absolute master of Bengal. Am I really so? Who is the real master? The English merchants. *Mir Kasim* is their slave; I am *Mir Kasim's* slave— I am, therefore, a slave of the real master's slave! Very exalted position after all! But why should I not be the master of Bengal? Who can stand before my guns? The English! O, if I could only meet them! But I shall never be the master unless the English are driven out of the country. I want to be the master of Bengal—I don't care for *Mir Kasim* in the least—I shall drag him down from the throne whenever I will like it. He is merely the step to my rising up to that exalted position. I have got up on the roof and can now throw down the ladder if I like, but the cursed English is the thorn on my way. They want to win over me and I want to gain over them. They will not come over to my side and so I shall drive them away. For the present let *Mir Kasim* be on the throne; siding with him, I shall blot out the name of the English from Bengal. This is why I am actively trying to pick up a quarrel with them. Afterwards, I shall dispense with *Mir Kasim*. This is the best course. But how is it that this letter comes to me so unexpectedly today? Why has this girl rushed into so bold an undertaking?"

Forthwith, the person of whom he was thinking came in, and stood before him. *Gurgan Khan* gave the visitor a special seat. It was *Dalani Begum* herself. *Gurgan Khan* said to her,

"I am very glad to see you tonight after a long time. I have not seen you since you got into the *Nawab's* harem. But why have you taken this rash step?"

Dalani. How is it rash?

Gurgan Khan. Being the *Nawab's Begum* you have stolen away from your place in the night, and have come to me alone—if the *Nawab* comes to know of it, he will surely put both of us to death.

Dalani. If he comes to know of it at all, I shall disclose our relation. Then surely he will have no reason to be angry.

Gurgan Khan. You are a mere girl and that is why you are so very confident of what you say. We have not disclosed our relation so long. Hitherto we have not told any one that we even know each other. Who will believe us if we speak of our relation in difficulty? Every one will take it as a means to escape. You should not have come.

Dalani. But how will the *Nawab* come to know of it? The sentinels are all obedient to you. They have allowed me to come here on my

BANKIM CHANDRA CHATTERJEE

showing them the badge you gave me. I have come to you to know something—is it true that there will be war with the English?

Gurgan Khan. Why, don't you hear of it from within the castle?

Dalani. Yes, I do. It is a rumour in the castle that war with the English is certain, and that you are bringing it about; why should you do so?

Gurgan Khan. You are a mere girl, how will you understand it?

Dalani. Am I speaking like a girl or do I act like a girl? When you have placed me in the *Nawab's seraglio* as your supporter, can you now ignore me as a girl?

Gurgan Khan. Let there be war. What loss shall you or I suffer from that? Let it break out if it will.

Dalani. Do you hope to win?

Gurgan Khan. Yes, there is every chance of our gaining the victory.

Dalani. Who has yet conquered the English?

Gurgan Khan. How many *Gurgan Khans* have the English encountered?

Dalani. *Seerajuddaulla* fancied the very same thing. However that may be, I am a woman and I believe in what the mind feels from within. It comes to my mind that we shall by no means be victorious in our fight with the English. This war will bring about our ruin. I have, therefore, come to entreat you not to encourage the idea of war.

Gurgan Khan. In a matter like this, woman's advice is not acceptable.

Dalani. You must accept my advice. O, save me—I see nothing but darkness all around!

Dalani then began to weep. *Gurgan Khan* was taken aback. He said, "Why should you weep? It does not matter if *Mir Kasim* is dethroned—I shall take you home along with me."

Dalani's eyes flashed fire. She said in a resentful tone, "Are you forgetting that *Mir Kasim* is my husband?"

Gurgan Khan was put out of countenance, and said, "No, I have not forgotten that. But then, one's husband is not immortal. If one husband is lost, another can be had. I have every hope that you will one day become the second *Noor Jahan* of India."

Dalani rose up. Checking her tears and dilating her eyes, she said, trembling with rage, "You go to hell. In an evil hour I came into this world as your sister—in an evil hour I promised to help you up. That woman has within herself affection, sympathy and a sense of piety, is a fact of which you are quite ignorant. If you desist from your counsel about the war, good and well. If not, my relation with you ceases henceforth. But why should there be no relation at all? From this day I shall bear to you the relation of an enemy. I shall take you to be my greatest enemy. Know it, I am your greatest, enemy. Bear in mind that in the royal *seraglio* your greatest enemy will live in my person." *Dalani* then rushed out of the mansion.

When *Dalani* got out, *Gurgan Khan* began to reflect. He felt that *Dalani* was no more his own—she was *Mir Kasim's*. She might have some affection for him as her brother, but she was far more affectionately attached to *Mir Kasim*. When she had come to know, or would come to know, that her brother was other than a well-wisher of her husband, she might do harm to the brother, for the good of the husband. So, she should not be allowed to re-enter the castle. *Gurgan Khan* called out the attendant. An armed retainer appeared before him. He sent orders through that man that the sentinels must not allow *Dalani* to get into the castle.

The messenger on horse-back reached the gate of the castle earlier. *Dalani* arrived there at the proper hour, and heard that her admission into the castle was prohibited. The news proved a terrible shock to her— she could no more remain standing—she gradually sat down on the ground, like a torn creeper. Tears came out of her eyes in torrents, and she exclaimed,

"Brother, you have deprived me of my only shelter in this world!"

"Let us go back to the commander's place," said *Kulsam*, in despair.

"You better go there. I shall have a place under the waves of the Ganges," replied *Dalani*, in grief and anger.

In that dark night, standing on the broad thoroughfare, *Dalani* began to weep. The stars were then glittering overhead, the sweet fragrance of blooming flowers was being diffused on all sides and the leaves of trees, enveloped in darkness were murmuring under a gentle breeze. *Dalani* in a voice of agony cried, "Kulsam!"

III

What Happened to Dalani

In the shade of night, *Dalani Begum*, standing on the broad thoroughfare, with only one maid about her, began to weep.

"What will you do now?" inquired *Kulsam*.

"Come, let us wait under that tree, till dawn," said *Dalani*, wiping away her tears.

Kulsam. If we be there till morning, we are sure to be arrested.

Dalani. What fear lies in that? What crime have I committed that I should fear?

Kulsam. We have stolen away from the castle like thieves—what has brought us out, you alone know. But just think, in what light the people will take it and what the *Nawab* will think of it.

Dalani. Let him take it in any light he pleases. God is my Judge—I know of no other tribunal. I shall die if I must—what harm is in that?

Kulsam. But what shall we gain by waiting there?

Dalani. I shall wait there to be arrested—that is my intention. Where shall they take me to?

Kulsam. To the *Durbar*.

Dalani. Before my lord? Ay, that is the place where I want to go. There is no other place for me to go to, in this world. If he orders my death, still, before the close of my life, I shall have an opportunity to tell him that I am not guilty. Let us better go and take our seat by the gate of the castle; for there we shall be noticed earlier.

At that moment, both of them saw with fear, in the darkness, the stalwart figure of a man, moving towards the Ganges. At this sight, they hid themselves in denser darkness under the tree. From there, they saw with greater fear that the stalwart man leaving the way to the Ganges, was coming towards them. At this, they concealed themselves in still thicker darkness.

The man, however, came there and said, "Who are you here, in this lonely place?" He then softly muttered, as if aside, "Who is there in this world so unfortunate, as keeping up nights in the streets, like me?"

The stature of the man had frightened the women, but his voice removed all fears—it was sweet and full of pity and sympathy. So *Kulsam* said,

"We are Women. Pray, who are you?"

"'We'? How many are you then?" inquired the man.

"We are only two", replied *Kulsam*.

"What are you doing here at this hour of the night?" he asked, in surprise.

Dalani then said, "We are two unlucky women—of what interest will our tale of sorrow be to you?"

"There are moments when even a most insignificant man can render help. If you are in trouble, let me know of it—I will help you to the extent of my capacity," replied the stranger gently.

Dalani. To help us out is almost an impossibility—who are you, please?

Stranger. "I am a humble man—only a poor *Brahmin* and an ascetic."

Dalani. Whoever you may be, your words are inspiring confidence in us. One, who is on the point of being drowned, cannot think of the fitness or unfitness of a support. But if you at all desire to know of our distress, please come away from the broad thoroughfare to a lonely place. In the night we cannot see if any one is within the reach of our voice. Our story is not to be told to any and every one.

"If that be so, just come along with me," said the ascetic, and he then proceeded towards the town with *Dalani* and *Kulsam*.

Arriving at the door of a small house, he knocked at it and called out, "*Ramcharan*."

Ramcharan opened the door from within. The ascetic asked him to strike a light. He lighted the lamp, and fell prostrate before the ascetic to pay his respects. The ascetic then asked him to go to bed. *Ramcharan* accordingly retired, after casting a glance at *Dalani* and *Kulsam*.

It is needless to say that, *Ramcharan* had no more sleep that night. "Why at this late hour of the night, the good hermit has brought in the two young women?" This thought became predominant in him. *Ramcharan* believed the ascetic to be a divine being—he knew that the hermit was the master of his passions; that belief was not shaken. At last, *Ramcharan* concluded, "Perhaps, the two women have just become widows—the good hermit has brought them here to induce them to burn themselves alive, on the funeral pyres of their deceased husbands— what a pity, I have taken so much time to understand this simple thing!"

The ascetic took his seat on a small piece of carpet—the women sat down on the floor. *Dalani* first disclosed herself, and then made a frank statement of what had happened in the night.

Hearing her, the ascetic thought within himself, "Who can prevent the inevitable? What will be, will be. But for all that, one should not lose heart and deny action—I must do what I should."

Alas, pious hermit! Why did you burn into ashes your valuable books? All books may be reduced to ashes, but the wonderful book of heart is proof against all fire.

The ascetic then said to *Dalani*, "My advice to you is, that you should not appear before the *Nawab*, all on a sudden. First, write to him what has happened, in details. If he still bears to you affection, he will surely believe your statement. You should appear before him when you get his permission."

"Who will carry my letter?" inquired *Dalani*.

"I will send it," was the good ascetic's kind reply.

Dalani then asked for paper, pen and ink.

The hermit again roused *Ramcharan*, who, as desired, brought in paper &c., and retired. *Dalani* began to write.

The hermit, in the meantime said, "This house is not mine, but stay here till you get the *Nawab's* permission—nobody will know of it and no one will ask you anything."

As there was no other alternative, *Dalani* agreed to his proposal. She finished the letter and handed it over to the hermit. He left with it, after he had given *Ramcharan* necessary instructions about the stay of *Dalani* and her maid in that house.

The hermit was well-known to the Hindu officers of the *Nawab*, at *Monghyr*. Even the Mahamedans knew him. So, he was respected by all the officers. *Ram Gobinda Roy*, who was the *Nawab's Munshi*, had great regard for him.

The hermit, entered into the castle, *at Monghyr*, after sunrise, and meeting *Ram Gobinda* there, handed over to him *Dalani's* letter to the *Nawab*.

"Don't mention my name. Simply say that the letter was brought by a *Brahmin*." he said, as he handed over the letter. "All right", said the *Munshi*. "Please come tomorrow for the reply." *Ram Gobinda*, however, could not know from whom the letter came. The hermit returned to the house, where he had left *Dalani* and *Kulsam*, and meeting the *Begum*, he said, "You will get the reply tomorrow. Some how or other manage to pass this day here."

In the morning *Ramcharan* found, to his great surprise, that no arrangements had been made for *Shahamaran*.

On the upper story of this house, there lay on a bed, a person, of whom we would now say something in the way of introduction. In painting his noble character, our pen, which has been profaned by the sins of *Shaibalini*, will be sanctified.

IV

Pratap

S undari had left *Shaibalini's Budgrow* really in great indignation. All the way she came crying shame on *Shaibalini*. She kept her husband agreeably engaged by calling *Shaibalini* by such sweet epithets as an ugly wretch, a vile shameless creature and a contemptible black-sheep. Returning home she wept much for *Shaibalini*. Later on, *Chandra Shekhar* came and deserted his home. After that, some days passed in the ordinary course. Nothing was heard of *Shaibalini* or *Chandra Shekhar*. It was then, that *Sundari* put on a *Dhakaishari* and sat down to wear her ornaments.

It has already been said that *Sundari* was the daughter of one of *Chandra Shekhar's* neighbours and was related to him as his cousin. Her father was not a poor man after all. For the most part, *Sundari* lived with her father. Her husband, *Sreenath*, although not exactly an abject dependent on his father-in-law, used to come and live in his house often. It has already been said that *Sreenath* had been at *Bedagram* when misfortune befell *Shaibalini*. In fact, *Sundari* was the mistress of the house. Her mother was an invalid and unfit for domestic duties. *Sundari* had a younger sister—her name was *Rupashi*. She, for the most part, lived in her father-in-law's house.

Sundari, putting on the *Dhakaishari* and wearing her ornaments said to her father, "I shall go to see *Rupashi*—I had a very bad dream about her." *Sundari's* father, *Krishna Kamal Chakravarti*, was very fond of his daughter. He at first tried to dissuade her, but ultimately gave his consent. *Sundari* left for *Rupashi's* father-in-law's house, and *Sreenath* for his own.

Who was *Rupashi's* husband? It was that *Pratap*! After *Chandra Shekhar* had married *Shaibalini*, he often used to meet her neighbour's son *Pratap*. *Chandra Shekhar* became much pleased with *Pratap's* nature. When *Sundari's* sister *Rupashi* attained marriageable age, *Chandra Shekhar* brought about her marriage with *Pratap*. Nor was that all. *Chandra Shekhar* was *Kasim Ali's* teacher—he had great influence with him; he was, therefore, able to secure for *Pratap* an employment in the *Nawab's* service. *Pratap's* merit lifted him up higher and higher every day. He is now a *Zemindar*. He has now got a palatial house of his own and is known all over the country. *Sundari's palanquin* entered into his mansion. On her arrival there, *Rupashi* made a respectful bow to her sister and conducted her in, with much cordiality. *Pratap* came there and greeted his sister-in-law warmly.

Afterwards *Pratap*, at an opportune moment, asked *Sundari* all about *Bedagram*. After other topics, he made enquiries about *Chandra Shekhar*.

"I have come here only to tell you all about *Chandra Shekhar*. Just hear me", said *Sundari* and then narrated in minute details all the circumstances relating to the disappearance of *Chandra Shekhar* and *Shaibalini*. *Pratap* was struck dumb in surprise.

Raising his head a little after, he said to *Sundari* in a rather harsh tone, "Why did you not inform me of this so long?"

Sundari. Why, for what good?

Pratap. For what good! You are a woman—I will not boast of my powers before you. I could be of some help, if I had been informed.

Sundari. How could I know that you would help?

Pratap. Why, don't you know that I owe every thing to *Chandra Shekhar*?

Sundari. Yes, I know it. But it is said that people forget their past when they become rich.

Pratap got annoyed—he became agitated and left the place without a word. *Sundari* was much delighted to find *Pratap* so angry.

On the next day *Pratap* left for *Monghyr* with only a cook and a servant. The name of the servant was *Ramcharan*. He left home without telling any one where he was going. To *Rupashi* only he said, "I am going in search of *Chandra Shekhar* and *Shaibalini*. I won't return till I find them out."

The house in which the hermit left *Dalani*, was *Pratap's* lodging, at *Monghyr*.

During the few days *Sundari* was with her sister, she abused *Shaibalini* to her heart's content. In morning, in noon and in evening, *Sundari* would adduce to *Rupashi* thousands of arguments to prove that *Shaibalini* was the greatest of world's sinners and the most unfortunate of her class.

One day *Rupashi* said, "Quite so, but then, why do you trouble yourself so much on her account?"

"Only to knock down her head—to send her to Death's door—to put fire into her mouth," replied *Sundari* in anger, but with feelings.

"Ah, sister you are very quarrelsome," remarked *Rupashi*.

"It is *Shaibalini* who has made me so," was *Sundari's* feeling reply.

V

On the Bank of the Ganges

The Council, at *Calcutta*, had decided to make war with the *Nawab*. For the present, they felt the necessity of sending some arms to the factory, at *Azimabad*. Accordingly a boat, loaded with arms, was despatched. It was also found necessary to send some private instructions to Mr. *Ellis*, the chief of the factory, at *Azimabad*. Mr. *Amyatt* was at *Monghyr* to settle all differences with the *Nawab*; no definite instructions could be given to *Ellis*, without knowing what *Amyatt* was doing there, and what he thought of the situation. So, an intelligent officer had to be sent to *Monghyr*. He would first see *Amyatt*, and taking necessary instructions from him, would go to *Ellis*, and explain to him the intentions of the *Calcutta* Council and those of *Amyatt*.

For this purpose, Governor *Vansittart* summoned *Foster* from *Purandarpur*. He would escort the boat carrying arms and proceed to *Patna*, after seeing *Amyatt*, at *Monghyr*. So, *Foster*, immediately after his arrival at *Calcutta*, had to leave for the western provinces. He had come to know of all these things before he left *Purandarpur*, and so he had already sent *Shaibalini* towards *Monghyr*.

Foster overtook *Shaibalini* in the way, and reached *Monghyr* with her and the boat carrying arms. He took leave of *Amyatt* after he had an interview with him. But just at that time, the boat loaded with arms was arrested under *Gurgan Khan's* orders. This gave rise to a controversy between *Amyatt* and the *Nawab*. One day, *Amyatt* and *Foster* decided that if the *Nawab* would let off the boat so much the better, or *Foster* would leave for *Patna* without it, the next morning.

Foster's two boats were lying fastened at the *Monghyr Ghat*. One of them was a country cargo boat—very big in size; the other was a *Budgrow*. On the cargo boat, some soldiers of the *Nawab* were on watch. There were also a few more of them on the bank. This boat was loaded with arms, and it was what *Gurgan Khan* meant to arrest.

The *Budgrow* contained no arms in it. It was lying some fifty cubits off the cargo boat. There was no sentinel of the *Nawab* on it. On its top, there was on watch, a *Telinga* sepoy of the English.

It was then past midnight. The night was dark but cloudless. The sentinel on the *Budgrow* was rising and sitting at intervals and dozing at times. There was a thick bush at the bank. From behind it, a person was closely observing some one at a distance. The observer was *Pratap Roy* himself.

Pratap saw that the sentinel was dozing. He, therefore, advanced and slowly got down in the river. The sentinel hearing a noise in the water, cried out, while dozing, "Who comes there?" *Pratap* gave no answer. The sentinel kept on dozing. Within the boat, *Foster* was awake and on alert. He heard the sentinel and looked around from within the *Budgrow*. He saw that a man had got down in the river—he thought, perhaps, to bathe.

At this moment, a report of a gun unexpectedly came from within the bush. The sentinel on the *Budgrow* was struck by a bullet and fell into the water. *Pratap* then moved to the spot, where the dark shadow of the boat had fallen and dipped himself into the water up to the chin. No sooner was the report of the gun heard, than the sepoys on the cargo boat shouted out, "What, ho!"

Those who were sleeping in the *Budgrow* now got up. *Foster* came out with his gun. He began to look around very closely. He found that the *Telinga* sepoy had disappeared. In the star-light, he could see his dead body floating away on the river. At first, he thought that it was the *Nawab's* sepoys who had killed him. But immediately after, he noticed a thin line of smoke, in the direction of the bush. Moreover, he saw that the men who were in the other boat were running up towards the *Budgrow*, to enquire what had happened. The stars were sparkling in the sky—lights were burning in the town—at the bank of the Ganges there were rows of boats, lying motionless in the darkness, like so many monsters, inert and lifeless in sleep—the ever-flowing *Bhagirathi* was running in murmurs—and in her current the corpse of the sentinel was floating away. *Foster* saw all these, in the twinkling of an eye.

Seeing the thin line of smoke above the bush, *Foster* raised his gun to fire in that direction. He could fully understand that the enemy was lying concealed in that bush. He could also feel that the hidden enemy who had killed the sentinel, might at any moment kill him as well. But he had come out to India after the battle of *Plassey*, and he could not believe that a native of Bengal would level his gun against an Englisnman. Besides, he thought that to an Englishman it was better to die than to fear an Indian foe. So, he had taken his stand there and raised his gun to fire. But instantly a flash of light was seen in the bush—a report of a gun was again heard—*Foster* was struck on the head and he fell into the water of the Ganges like the sentinel. His gun fell on the boat with a noise.

At that moment, *Pratap*, taking out a knife from his waist, cut down the ropes with which the *Budgrow* was fastened at the bank. The water was very shallow there and the current being very mild, the boatmen had not cast down the anchor. Even if it had been dropped down, it would have mattered very little to the strong and swift-handed *Pratap*, who briskly jumped upon the *Budgrow*, as soon as the ropes were cut off.

All these happened within a time which is only a hundredth part of what has been taken in describing them. The fall of the sentinel, *Foster's* appearance on the top of the *Budgrow*, his fall from and *Pratap's* getting on it—all these had taken place before the men from the other boat could come there.

When they arrived at the spot, they found that the *Budgrow* had been shifted to deep waters by *Pratap's* skill. One of them made an attempt to swim up to the *Budgrow* to get hold of it. *Pratap* raising a pole, struck him with it, on the head. The man swam back—no one else ventured to advance. Touching the bottom of the river with that pole, *Pratap* propelled the boat. The *Budgrow*, taking a side turn, came upon the strong current, and moved towards the east, in great speed. With the pole in hand, *Pratap* turned back and found that another Telinga sepoy, kneeling down on the top of the *Budgrow*, was raising his gun to fire at him. *Pratap* struck the sepoy on his hand, with the pole. His hand became disabled, and the gun dropped down. *Pratap* picked up that gun and also the one which had fallen down from *Foster's* hand. He then spoke aloud to the men in the boat,

"Know it, my name is *Pratap Roy*. Even the *Nawab* is afraid of me. With these two guns and the pole, I can alone kill all of you. If you obey me, I shall not harm any one of you. I am going to the helm—let the boatmen all row—others should remain where they are now; death is certain if they move, otherwise they have nothing to fear."

Pratap, then, poked the boatmen with the end of the pole, and made them go to the oars. They were struck with fear, and began to row. *Pratap* came to the helm. No one, after that, ventured to speak or question. The *Budgrow* moved on swiftly. There were some fires from the cargo boat, but as it was impossible to see, in the star-light, the person to be aimed, they were immediately stopped.

Then, some men, armed with guns, came out, in a small boat, to seize the *Budgrow*. At first *Pratap* did nothing. But when they came to close quarters, he let both of his guns go off at them. Two were wounded—the rest turned back their boat out of fear and rowed away in all haste.

Ramcharan, who lay concealed in the bush, finding that *Pratap* was out of danger, and that the sepoys were coming from the cargo boat to make a search in the bush, made himself scarce.

VI

THE THUNDERBOLT

In that boat, moving under the shade of the night, on the dark bosom of the flowing *Bhagirathi*, rose from sleep—*Shaibalini*.

There were two cabins in the *Budgrow*—*Foster* occupied one and *Shaibalini* with her maid the other. Even then, *Shaibalini* had not dressed herself out as an English lady. She had put on a black bordered *Shari* and had worn bangles and anklets after the Indian fashion. She had with her *Parbati*, that very maid of *Purandarpur*. *Shaibalini* had been sleeping. While asleep she was dreaming that the water of the familiar *Bhima* pond was edged by a thin line of darkness, cast upon it by those trees on the bank, which stooped their boughs, as if, eager to embrace its watery bosom, and that *Shaibalini* herself was floating there, with only her face above the water, transformed into a lily; she saw that a golden swan was gliding about at one extremity of the pond and a white boar moving around on the mounds; *Shaibalini* was anxious to get hold of the beautiful swan, but the golden bird, she fancied, was turning away from her in neglect—the boar, it seemed, was roaming there in quest of the lily-like *Shaibalini*. The face of the swan could not be seen but that of the boar, as it appeared, resembled *Foster's*. *Shaibalini* felt, she was trying to go after the swan to catch it, but her legs, being transformed into films of lotus, got rooted to the bed of the pond—she lost the power of moving; the boar on the other hand seemed to say, "Come to me, I will get the swan you want."

Shaibalini awoke at the first report of the gun—then she heard the noise with which the sentinel fell on the water. In the langour of disturbed sleep, *Shaibalini* for a time could not understand what the matter was. The swan and the boar were still reccuring to her mind. When another gun was heard and a great row was created on the bank, her sleep was completely broken. She came out in the outer cabin, and for a time looked out through the slightly opened door—but she failed to make out anything. She then returned to the inner cabin and found that *Parbati* also had awakened. *Shaibalini* asked her,

"Can you say what's the matter?"

Parbati. No, nothing at all. But, from what the people outside are saying, it seems, *Dacoits* have come upon our boat. The *Sahib* has been killed—alas, it is the result of our sins!

Shaibalini. The *Sahib* has been killed, how can that be the result of our sins? It is rather the consequence of his own wickedness.

Parbati. The *Dacoits* are upon us—it is we alone who are in danger.

Shaibalini. Wherein lies the danger? We have been with one *Dacoit* and it makes little difference if we have to accompany another. Won't it be better if we get out of the clutches of a white bandit and fall into the hands of a black one?

So saying, *Shaibalini*, waving her beautiful braid, hanging over her back from her little faultless head, smiled a gentle smile and took her seat on a little bedstead.

"In a moment like this I can hardly endure that smile of yours," said *Parbati*.

Shaibalini. If you can't bear it, better drown yourself in the river—the water of the Ganges is deep enough. The time has come when I should smile and so smile I must. Do go out and call before me one of the pirates—I would like to have a talk with him. *Parbati* got annoyed and said, "We shall not have to call them in—they will come here of their own accord."

But nearly two hours passed, yet none of the pirates came in. *Shaibalini* then sadly observed, "Ah me, how ill-fated are we! Even the *Dacoits* do not take any notice of us." *Parbati* was trembling with fear.

After a rather long time the boat arrived at a *Char*. After it had stopped there for a while some *Lathials*, armed with clubs, came there, with a *palanquin*—*Ramcharan* was leading them. The carriers placed the *palanquin* on the bank. *Ramcharan* got upon the *Budgrow* and came to *Pratap*. He then entered into the cabin with necessary instructions from *Pratap*. He first looked at *Parbati's* face and then saw *Shaibalini*. To her he said, "Pray alight here."

"Who are you—where am I to go?" inquired *Shaibalini*.

"I am your servant—you have nothing to fear," replied *Ramcharan*. "Please come along with me—the *Sahib* is killed."

After this *Shaibalini* did not say anything. She rose up and followed *Ramcharan*. She alighted from the *Budgrow* along with him. *Parbati* was following her, but she was stopped by *Ramcharan*. She remained in the boat out of fear. *Shaibalini* got into the *palanquin*, as asked by *Ramcharan*, who led it to *Pratap's* lodging.

　　　　　　　　BANKIM CHANDRA CHATTERJEE

Even then *Dalani* and *Kulsam* were putting up at *Pratap's* place. *Ramcharan* did not take *Shaibalini* into their room, lest their sleep were disturbed. He conducted her to an upstairs apartment, and after lighting a lamp there, asked her to take rest. He then made his obeisance to *Shaibalini*, and departed, closing the door of the room from out-side,

"Whose house is this?" inquired *Shaibalini* of *Ramcharan*, as he was leaving the room. *Ramcharan* turned a deaf ear to the query and left the place.

Ramcharan had brought *Shaibalini* to *Pratap's* house at his own discretion—*Pratap* had instructed him otherwise. He had directed *Ramcharan* to take the *palanquin* to *Jagat Sett's* place. In the way *Ramcharan* thought within himself, "Is there any possibility of my finding, at this hour of the night, *Jagat Sett's* gate open? Even if I find it open, will the porters allow me to get into the house now? If I am asked to state all particulars, what shall I say? Should I give out everything to risk an arrest as a murderer? No, that can't be; for the present it is better to go to our own place." So thinking, *Ramcharan* conducted the *palanquin* to their own house.

Now, *Pratap*, finding that the *palanquin* was out of sight, alighted from the boat. Every one in *Foster's Budgrow* had already become quiet and silent seeing the gun in *Pratap's* hand, and now no body dared speak out seeing the *Lathials* at his beck and call. Alighting from the *Budgrow*, *Pratap* proceeded towards his own house. Arriving at the gate, he knocked at it—*Ramcharan* opened the door from within. The very moment he stepped in, *Pratap* heard from *Ramcharan* that he had acted contrary to his directions. This annoyed *Pratap* a little. He said to *Ramcharan*, "There is yet time, take her along with you to *Jagat Sett's* place—go, get her down.

Ramcharan went up and found—people will be surprised to hear—that *Shaibalini* was sleeping. Sleep is not possible at such a time. Whether it is possible or not, is more than what we can say—we are simply recording what actually happened. *Ramcharan* did not wake her up. He returned to *Pratap* and said, "She is sleeping—should I call her up?" *Pratap* was astonished to hear this—he said within himself, "The learned *Chanakya* forgot to notice that a woman sleeps sixteen times more than a man." He then said to *Ramcharan*, "No, you need not go so far. You too go to sleep—we have had enough of toil—I would also now take some rest."

Ramcharan then retired for rest. There was yet some night left. In the house—in the town outside it—in fact everywhere—silence and darkness prevailed. *Pratap* went upstairs alone and noiselessly. He proceeded towards his bed-room and arriving at the door he opened it. To his surprise he found that *Shaibalini* was lying there on a sofa. *Ramcharan* had forgotten to say that he had left *Shaibalini* in the very bed-room of *Pratap*.

In the light of the burning lamp *Pratap* saw, as if, some one had heaped on the white bed, blooming flowers of the whitest glow—as if, some one had floated smiling snow-white lilies on the unruffled expanse of the silvery waters of the Ganges. What a placid fascinating beauty it was! *Pratap* could not at once turn away his eyes from so captivating a sight. It was not that *Pratap* lost himself in the fascination of that beauty or became a slave of his senses, that he could not turn away his eyes, but it was in abstraction that he gazed at that beautiful spectacle like a spellbound spectator. Thousand remembrances of a distant past came into his mind—all on a sudden the depth of his memory was stirred up, and waves of recollections began to strike themselves one against another.

Shaibalini had not fallen asleep. She was but reflecting on her situation, with her eyes closed. Finding her in that position *Ramcharan* had concluded that she had been sleeping. In her deep abstraction, *Shaibalini* could not hear the footsteps of *Pratap* when he entered the room. *Pratap* had come upstairs with the gun in hand. He now placed the gun against the wall. He was then in a state of forgetfulness and so the gun had not been carefully placed; it slipped and fell down on the floor. *Shaibalini* opened her eyes at the noise, and saw *Pratap*. She sat up on the bed, rubbed her eyes, and exclaimed with emotion,

"Oh, what I see! Who are you?" She could say no more—she fainted and fell on the bed.

Pratap instantly fetched water and began to sprinkle it on the face of *Shaibalini*. Her face now wore the charming beauty of a sweet bedewed lily. The water wetted her handsome locks, uncurled them and then trickled down in drops. Her tresses looked as beautiful as mosses hanging from a lotus.

Shaibalini soon recovered her consciousness. *Pratap* stood up. *Shaibalini* then very calmly asked,

"Who are you? Is it *Pratap* or some angel has come to deceive me?"

Pratap. "Yes, I am *Pratap*."

Shaibalini. When I was in the boat I once thought that I heard your voice. But instantly I felt that it was a mere illusion. I had then just risen from sleep in the midst of a dream and so I thought it to be only a delusion of my mind.

Shaibalini then breathed a deep sigh and was silent. *Pratap* found that *Shaibalini* had fully recovered, and was, therefore, about to leave the room, without a word, when *Shaibalini* entreated him not to go away. *Pratap* stopped against his will.

"Why have you come here?" then inquired *Shaibalini*.

"This is my lodging," was *Pratap's* brief reply.

Shaibalini in fact had not fully regained the usual calmness of her mind—her heart was burning within herself, as if on fire—even her nails were quivering. Each particular hair of her body stood up on its end. She remained silent for some time and picking up a little strength, asked,

"Who brought me here?"

Pratap. We have brought you here.

Shaibalini. "We"! Who are the persons, *Pratap*?

Pratap. My servant and myself.

Shaibalini. Why have you brought me here, and for what purpose?

Pratap got much annoyed and said in an angry tone, "No one should see the face of a sinner like you. We have rescued you from the hands of a wicked alien, yet you question why we have brought you here!"

Shaibalini did not show temper at *Pratap's* outburst. With a trembling voice, almost weeping, she gently said, "If you had considered my living with an alien under the same roof to be my misfortune, why did you not kill me in the boat? You had guns with you."

Pratap got more annoyed and said, rather haughtily, "I would have done that—I refrained from it only because it is a great sin to kill a woman; but for you death is better than life."

Shaibalini wept. Checking her tears a little after, she said, "True it is that death is preferable to life in my case—let people say what they like, but you should not say so. Who has reduced me to this woeful condition? You. Who has made my life dark and gloomy? It is you *Pratap*. For whom have I, being disappointed in my pleasant hopes, become so reckless? For you. For whom am I so miserable? For you alone. Again, for whom could I not like my home and live a steady domestic life? It is only for you *Pratap*. You should not rebuke me."

Pratap. I scold you because you are a sinner. You make me responsible for your evil deeds! God knows, I am not guilty of any sin. He knows that of late I used to dread you as a serpent and I have all along kept myself out of your path. I deserted *Bedagram* in fear of your venom. Sin is in your heart and in your sentiments—you have fallen from grace and so you blame me. What harm have I done you?

"What harm have you done?" roared out *Shaibalini*, trembling in violent agitation. "Why did you again appear before me with the matchless beauty of your etherial mould? Why did you kindle before my eyes the fascinating light of that beauty, when I was just stepping into youth? Why did you revive in me, the memory of what I had forgotten? Why I happened to see you at all? If I had seen you, why did I not get you as my own? If that were to be so, why did not death come upon me? Don't you know that it was your thought which made my home a wilderness? Need I tell you, that I deserted my home in the hope that, although I am torn away from you, I may one day have you as my own? Or else, what is *Foster* to me?"

Shaibalini's words violently shocked *Pratap*—he felt as if a thunderbolt had come upon him—he rushed out of the room in agony, like one stung by scorpions.

At that moment a great noise was heard at the gate of the house.

VII

GOLSTON AND JOHNSON

When *Ramcharan* had alighted from the boat with *Shaibalini* and quitted with her, and *Pratap* too had left, the *Telinga* sepoy, who had been sitting on the top of the boat, with his hands benumbed at *Pratap's* strike, stealthily alighted from the boat and got upon the bank of the river. He then followed the track which formed the route of *Shaibalini's palanquin*. He kept an eye on the *palanquin* from at a great distance, and began to follow it unnoticed. The sepoy was a *Mahomedan* by race. His name was *Bakaulla Khan*. The first batch of soldiers, that came to Bengal with *Clive*, was recruited in *Madras*, and for that reason, in those days, all the native soldiers of the English, in Bengal, were styled as *Telingas*. At the time of this story, many up-country *Hindus* and *Mahomedans* were taken into the English army. *Bakaullah* was an inhabitant of a place in the neighbourhood of *Gazipur*.

Bakaullah followed the *palanquin* unobserved as far as *Pratap's* lodging. He saw that *Shaibalini* entered into that house, and immediately left for *Amyatt's* quarters. On his arrival there he noticed considerable agitation in the camp. *Amyatt* had already heard what happened in *Foster's Budgrow*. *Bakaullah* came to know that *Amyatt* had promised a reward of a thousand rupees to any one who would find out the rowdy oppressors, on that very night. *Bakaullah* went to *Amyatt* and reported to him everything in detail. He said, "I can point out the house of the offenders." At this *Amyatt's* countenance became cheerful, and his contracted eyebrows became straight again. He ordered four sepoys and a native officer to accompany *Bakaullah*. "Go, and drag the ruffians here before me," then said he with all the weight of his authority.

"In that case, pray, order two Englishmen to accompany me—*Pratap Roy* is Satan incarnate—no native of this country will be able to arrest him," urged *Bakaullah* persuasively. Two armed Englishmen—*Golston* and *Johnson*—set out with *Bakaullah*, at *Amyatt's* command.

"Did you ever go within that house?" inquired *Golston* and *Johnson* of *Bakaullah*, just as they were starting.

"No—I did not," replied *Bakaullah*.

"Then, take with you a candle and a match—the *Hindus* do not keep up light throughout the night for fear of expense," said *Golston* to *Johnson*.

Johnson took with him, in his pocket, a candle and a match box. The two Englishmen then proceeded along the broad thoroughfare, with firm and steady steps, resembling those of the soldiers marching on to the battle-field. Neither of them said a word. The four sepoys and the native officer with *Bakaullah* were following them silently. The watchmen of the town turned aside in fear before them. *Golston* and *Johnson*, with the sepoys, noiselessly arrived at the gate of *Pratap's* house, and gently knocked at the door.

As a servant *Ramcharan* had no equal. He was a trained hand in securing ease and comfort to his master by artfully rubbing his body and applying oil to it before bath. He was an expert in handsomely frilling his master's *Dhuties* and was an excellent valet. As a keeper of household furniture, he had no equal—a marketeer like him was rare. But these were his ordinary qualifications. He was well-known throughout the length and breadth of *Murshidabad* as a trained and skilful stick-player—Many *Hindus* and *Mahomedans* had met their death at his hands. As to how sharp and infallible he was at his rifle, was written in unmistakable letters on the waters of the Ganges with *Foster's* blood.

But *Ramcharan* had still one more qualification, which was more useful than all these, at times of emergency—this was his cunningness. *Ramcharan* was as sly as a fox. Nevertheless, his devotion to his master and his trustworthiness were unrivalled.

When *Ramcharan* came to open the door, he thought within himself, "Who is it that knocks at this ungodly hour? Is it the pious hermit? Most likely so. But we have had quite an adventure tonight, and I am not going to open the door at this unearthly hour, till I see who knocks at it."

Ramcharan then noiselessly came up to the entrance and stood there for a while in silence—he was listening to something. He heard two men whispering to each other in a peculiar language—*Ramcharan* used to call it "*Indil mindil*"—now people call it "English." At this *Ramcharan* said within himself, "Wait you devils! If I must open the door, I must do so with a gun in hand. He must be a damned fool who trusts in "*Indil mindil*."

Ramcharan also thought that, perhaps, one gun was not sufficient and that he should call up his master. So he came away from the gate to call up *Pratap*.

Now the Englishmen lost their patience. "We need not wait any more," cried *Johnson* fretfully, unable to endure the delay. "Kick at the door, the Indian door will not stand British kicks."

Golston kicked at the door—it cracked, jarred and made a rattling noise. *Ramcharan* ran. The noise reached *Pratap's* ears. He began to descend the stairs to come down. The door did not break at that kick. Then *Johnson* kicked at it and it gave way.

"Let, in this way whole India crumble down under British kicks," vaunted forth the Englishmen and entered into the house—the sepoys followed them in.

Pratap met *Ramcharan* on the stairs. "Hide yourself in the darkness—some Englishmen have come, perhaps, from *Ambat's* camp," whispered *Ramcharan* to *Pratap*.

Ramcharan would pronounce *Amyatt* as *Ambat*.

Pratap. What fear is in that?

Ramcharan. Mind you, they are eight in number.

Pratap. What will be the fate of the women in this house if I hide myself like a coward? Go, and bring down my gun.

If *Ramcharan* had known all particulars about the English, he would not have asked *Pratap* to hide himself in the darkness. By the time they were speaking to each other, the house suddenly became lighted. *Johnson* handed over to a sepoy the burning taper. In its light the Englishmen saw two persons standing on the stairs.

"What, are those the ruffians?" inquired *Johnson* of *Bakaullah*.

Bakaullah could not recognise them fully. He had seen *Pratap* and *Ramcharan* in the darkness of night, and so it was not possible for him to identify them with confidence. But the pain of his broken hand had passed endurance—some one, it does not matter who, is responsible for it. *Bakaullah*, therefore, said,

"Yes, they are indeed."

The Englishmen then leaped upon the stairs like tigers. Finding the sepoys following them, *Ramcharan* began to ascend the stairs, in a breathless speed, to fetch *Pratap's* gun. *Johnson* noticed him. He instantly raised the pistol in his hand and fired at *Ramcharan*. The shot struck one of his legs and he sat down, disabled to move any further.

Pratap had no arms with him—he was unwilling to run away; besides, he saw with his own eyes the fate of *Ramcharan* in his attempt to get away. *Pratap*, therefore, calmly asked the Englishmen,

"Who are you—why have you come here?"

"Who are you?" interposed *Golston* haughtily.

"I am *Pratap Roy*," responded *Pratap* with his characteristic calmness.

Bakaullah had not forgotten that name. From the top of *Foster's Budgrow, Pratap*, with gun in hand, had boastingly said, "Know it, my name is *Pratap Roy.*" *Bakaullah* at once cried out, "Sir, this man is the ring-leader."

Thereupon *Johnson* caught hold of *Pratap's* one hand and *Golston* the other. *Pratap* felt that it was useless to apply strength. He endured every thing silently. The native officer had a handcuff with him. He put it on to *Pratap's* hands.

"What's to be done with that fellow?" asked *Golston* of *Johnson*, pointing out with his finger the wounded *Ramcharan*.

"Bring that man along with you," enjoined *Johnson* upon two sepoys.

The sepoys accordingly dragged away *Ramcharan* along with them.

The noise roused *Dalani* and *Kulsam* from their sleep, and greatly frightened them. They slightly opened the door of their room and were seeing through the opening what was going on outside. Their room was close to the stairs.

When the Englishmen were coming down with *Pratap* and *Ramcharan*, the light of the burning taper in the hand of the sepoy, accidentally fell upon *Dalani's* dark blue eyes, moving about the opening of the door. *Bakaullah* happened to catch a glimpse of those eyes. The moment he saw them, he cried out, "Here is *Mr. Foster's* lady."

"Oh I see! Where is she?" said *Golston* in pleasant surprise.

"In that room," replied *Bakaullah*, pointing out with his finger the slightly opened door, through which *Dalani* was peeping.

Johnson and *Golston* entered into the room and asked *Dalani* and *Kulsam* to follow them.

Dalani and *Kulsam* were greatly frightened and confounded. They followed the Englishmen quietly.

Shaibalini alone remained in that house. She too had seen everything.

VIII

The Strange Ways of Sin

Like the *Mahomedan* girls, *Shaibalini* had also been peeping through the slightly opened door of her room. All the three were women and so all of them were affected with the feeling of curiosity which is common to their class. Again, all the three were sick with fear, and it is the characteristic of fear that it excites in one, the desire of repeatedly seeing the object of fear. *Shaibalini*, therefore, had seen every thing from start to finish. When all left, *Shaibalini* found that she was alone in that house, and began to reflect. She thought within herself, "What should I do now; I am alone, but what need I fear in that? I have nothing on earth to be afraid of. There is nothing more horrible than death itself, and what can there be to frighten a soul that always seeks death? But then, why that death does not come upon me? It is very easy to commit suicide—is it actually so? Stay! Let me consider. I had been on the river for many days, but could I drown myself in the water on any day? If I had stolen away from the boat in the night, when all fell asleep, and plunge into the water, who could detect me? Yes, I would have been detected—the sentinels on the boat used to keep watch by night. But then, I made no attempt. I had the will but I did not try to give effect to it. Even then I had hope, and no one can court death when there is hope. But what hope is there for me today? This is verily the day when I should take leave of this world. But *Pratap* has been taken away in chains—I cannot die till I come to know of his fate. Why should I be at all anxious to know of it? Let it be what it will—it concerns me not. I am a sinner in his eyes—what, then, is *Pratap* to me? I know it not, but this much I know that he is the blazing fire and I am the charmed fly—in the long and dreary path of this world he is to me summer's first flash of lightning—he is my death. Oh, why did I get away with an alien? Oh, why did I not return home with *Sundari*?"

Shaibalini slapped her forehead in repentance, and began to weep. The house at *Bedagram*, once her home, came into her recollection. The memory of the familiar spot by the side of the wall of the compound, where *Shaibalini* had planted with her own hands the *Karabi* tree, came into her mind—how the topmost branch of that tree, once her object of love and care, towering above the wall, used to swing to and fro with the red flowers on it, as if, anxious to touch the blue vault of the sky—how sometimes bees and little birds used to come and rest on it! The sacred *Tulashi*—the neat and clean space around it—the pet cat, the talking bird in the cage and the stalwart mango tree by the side of the house—all appeared in her mind one by one in the vividness of reality. Thousand other things came into her recollection. Oh, how agreeable was her situation when from the roof of her house, at *Bedagram*, she used to see every evening various delightful and charming aspects of the blue serene sky; how pleasant it was for her to fill everyday, for *Chandra Shekhar's* use, at the time of worship, the flower basket with numerous sweet-scented, snow-white blooming flowers, moistened by her with pure water! Again, how happy was she when she used to breathe every evening the gentle, refreshing, fragrant breeze on the mounds of the familiar *Bhima* tank; how charming were the gleaming wavelets she used to see there—how captivating was the flowing melody of the cuckoo from the trees around! *Shaibalini* breathed a deep sigh. She thought, "It was my hope that I would see *Pratap* if I would only get away from home; I thought that I would again return to the factory at *Purandarpur*, which is close to *Pratap's* house, and from the window of my room I would make *Pratap* a captive to my glance. Then, at an opportune moment I would give *Foster* the slip and throw myself at *Pratap's* feet. I was a bird in the cage and so I knew nothing of the ways of this world. I did not know that man proposes and God disposes. Again, I did not know that the cage of the English was made of steel and it was beyond my power to break through it. Oh, in vain have I brought disgrace upon me—I have lost my caste and spoiled my future life!"

Strange, it did not occur to wicked *Shaibalini* that there is nothing like success or failure in respect of sin—rather failure is better than success; but a day came when she realised this truth—a day came when she prepared herself to sacrifice even her life for her redemption. Had that not been the case, we would not have introduced to our readers this sinful character.

Shaibalini continued to reflect as before. She said, "My future life? Ah me, its prospects were marred on the very day I first saw *Pratap*. God, who can read through our minds, must have ordained my damnation on that very day. Even in this world I am in hell—my mind is hell itself; or why am I suffering so much pain and affliction? If it is not so, how is it that I passed this long time with *Foster*, who is verily my eyesore? Nor is that all. Perhaps evil betides all that is good and dear to me. It is, perhaps, on my account that *Pratap* is now in danger—oh! why did I not put an end to my life?" *Shaibalini* began to weep again. After a while she wiped away her tears. She contracted her eyebrows and began to bite her lips; for a time her smiling lily-like face wore the fearful appearance of an angry snake. "Why did I not put an end to my life?" repeated *Shaibalini*, and took off from her waist a bagnet, which contained a sharp pointed knife. She then took the knife in her hand and began to feel its sharp edge with her finger. She said, "Did I carry this knife with me in vain? Why have I not so long pierced my wretched heart with it? Why? Only because I lost myself in the fascination of my hopes. But now!" Forthwith, as she concluded, *Shaibalini* placed on her breast the fore-end of the knife. She kept it there in that position, and said within herself, "On another day I placed this knife in the very same way on the breast of sleeping *Foster*. On that day I could not stab him to death for want of courage, and this day too my heart fails to commit suicide. The dread of this knife subdued even wicked *Foster*—he had felt that if he would enter into my cabin, this knife would either end his life or mine. The fear of this knife brought under restraint the turbulent Englishman, but my unruly heart has not yielded to its influence. Should I commit suicide now? No, not today. If I must die, I shall court death when I go back to *Bedagram*. I shall not end my life till I meet *Sundari* and tell her that although I have lost my caste and have been excommunicated from society, I am not guilty of a particular crime. And he—who is my husband—what shall I say to him at the time of my death? Oh! I cannot think of it. The very thought of it gives me unbearable pain—it makes me feel, as if, countless scorpions are stinging me, and liquid fire is flowing through all my veins? I have forsaken him because I am not worthy of him. Has that pained him in any way? Has he lamented for me? Perhaps not—I am not near and dear to him. His books are all in all with him. He then cannot lament for me. Oh, I wish someone would come from *Bedagram* and tell me so, and also report to me as to how he is doing and what he is about! I have never loved him and I will never love him, yet if I have hurt his feelings, I have undoubtedly made the burden of my sins heavier. I earnestly desire to tell him one thing—but *Foster* is dead and who will bear testimony to what I intend to say? Oh! who will believe me?" *Shaibalini* then laid herself on the bed she was sitting upon, and remained absorbed in thoughts, as before. She fell asleep early in the morning, and saw many unpleasant dreams in her sleep. When she woke up, the sun had risen far above the horizon and its shooting rays had made their ways into the room through the opened window. What *Shaibalini* saw before her, when she opened her eyes, startled, frightened and paralysed her. She saw *Chandra Shekhar*!

PART III
THE TOUCH OF VIRTUE

I

RAMANANDA SWAMI

There had been living, for some days, a *Paramahansa* in a monastery, at *Monghyr*. His name was *Ramananda Swami*. The good hermit, whom we have spoken of before, was conferring with him in a very humble and respectful manner. Many believed that *Ramananda Swami* had, by spiritual exercises, freed himself from the fetters of flesh and blood and could hold communion with the spirit-world. However that may be, he was undoubtedly a man of unrivalled knowledge and wisdom. The common belief of the time was that he alone knew the dead philosophies and sciences of ancient India. He said,

"Listen to me dear *Chandra Shekhar*! you must always carefully apply the sciences which you have learnt from me. And do not under any circumstance give *sorrow* a place in your heart. I say so because in this world there is no distinct reality as *sorrow*. To the wise, *happiness* and *sorrow* are one and the same thing. If you make a distinction between them, then those who are universally known as happy or virtuous shall have to be said to have been unhappy throughout their life."

After this *Ramananda Swami* briefly referred to the anecdotes of *Jajati, Harish Chandra, Dasharatha* and some other ancient kings. He then alluded to the events of the life of *Sree Ram Chandra, Judhisthir, Nala* and some other great kings of high eminence. He proved that those pious kings were unhappy throughout their life—they were seldom happy. He then briefly related the incidents of the life of *Bashistha, Biswamitra* and other great sages of sacred *Hindusthan*, and proved that they were always unhappy. He next referred to the cursed and persecuted gods like *Indra*, and showed that even the celestial beings were not free from sorrow. Lastly, calling up his heart-captivating heaven-born power of speech, he began to examine the unknown, the unknowable and the infinite mind of the Great Creator. He said with magic eloquence, "God, who is omniscient, must have been perceiving in His mind the endless sorrow of the endless universe, through endless time. Is it possible that He, who is all-merciful, perceives in His mind the immense sorrows of this universe and yet does not feel unhappy on that account, or how can He be all-merciful? Mercy is inseparably associated with the feeling of sorrow—the existence of the one necessarily means the existence of the other. Therefore, God, who is merciful, is unhappy through eternity, on account of the eternal sorrows of the unlimited universe; or He is not merciful! You may ask, how can He suffer from sorrow when He is not affected by any influence, in spite of His universal consciousness? The answer will be, that He who is immovable is certainly unconcerned in the great work of creation, preservation and destruction, and so He cannot be accepted as the creator and the dispenser. If there be any one as a creator and a dispenser, He can by no means be said to be indifferent and impassive—He is full of sorrow. But that cannot be as well; for He is ever joyful. The inference, therefore, is irresistible that there is no such thing as *sorrow*. On the other hand if the existence of sorrow is admitted, are there no means to prevent this all-pervading misery? No, there is none. But if we all set ourselves to the mitigation of each other's distress then certainly the existence of sorrow can be done away with. Just see that the Creator himself is always busy in removing the sorrows and afflictions of His creation. The mitigation of the misery of this world removes the sorrows of the Divine mind. All the deities of heaven are also continually engaged in removing the pains and sufferings of the animal world, and that affords contentment to them; or else those heavenly beings, who are not transmutable by passions and emotions, would have no pleasure or happiness." Then *Ramananda Swami* eulogised, with fervent eloquence, the ancient sages for their active love of mankind and alluded in graceful terms of praise to the beneficent self-abnegations of heroes like the great *Bhisma*. He proved in a convincing manner that he alone is happy who lives for others, and none else. He then extolled, times without number, the noble virtue of philanthropy and benevolence. He traversed the Scriptures, the *Vedas* and the Mythologies and cited from them, in unbroken eloquence, numerous instances in support of his arguments. To emphasise them he ransacked the vast stock of words and gave accent to a long and unbroken series of phrases and phraseologies, agreeable to the ear and pregnant with deep meanings—he plundered the invaluable treasure of literature and eloquently poured forth poem after poem, rich with deep thoughts, happy sentiments and flowery rhetorics. Above all, he cast upon the mind of his hearer the enchanting halo of his genuine love of virtue. Those rare and wonderful words, accentuated in a silvery tone, with skilful intonations, resounded in *Chandra Shekhar's* ears like the sound of a trumpet. Sometimes, it seemed, they resembled the roaring thunder and again they made a delightful music for the ears, as soft and sweet as the melody which flows from a lute! The hermit was struck with admiration and became spell-bound. His hairs stood up on their ends. He rose up and made a profound obeisance to *Ramananda Swami*. He said, "My noble preceptor! I am now initiated in your faith, and from this day forth I shall be guided by the gospels you have preached to me. *Ramananda Swami* embraced *Chandra Shekhar*.

II

The New Acquaintance

Now, *Dalani's* letter, which was carried by the good hermit, was duly laid before the *Nawab*. The *Nawab* thus came to know *Dalani's* whereabouts. *Palanquins* were sent to *Pratap's* house to bring *Dalani* and *Kulsam*.

The day had far advanced then. In that house there was none but *Shaibalini*. The *Nawab's* men saw her and concluded that she was the *Begum*.

Shaibalini heard that she was to go to the castle. All on a sudden an evil intention sprang up in her mind. The poets forget themselves in their eulogy of *hope*. And no doubt, *hope* is often the source of many pleasures and enjoyments of this world; but at the same time, it is *hope* which is the origin of sorrow and misery. All crimes are committed in the hope of gain. Only good works are done without any expectation of return. Those, who perform noble deeds for the golden prospects in heaven, cannot be said to have been doing good works. It was hope which completely captivated *Shaibalini*, and made her get into the *Nawab's palanquin* without any hesitation.

A eunuch attendant brought *Shaibalini* within the castle and ushered her into the Royal presence, in the *Seraglio*. The *Nawab* found to his surprise that she was not *Dalani*—he also noticed that even *Dalani* was not so striking a beauty as the fair stranger before him. In fact, he felt that in his harem there was no lady who wore so captivating a beauty! The *Nawab* asked,

"Who are you, fair lady?"

Shaibalini. I am a *Brahmin's* daughter.

Nawab. Why have you come here?

Shaibalini. The Royal attendants have brought me here.

Nawab. They have done so, mistaking you for the *Begum*. Why has not the *Begum* come?

Shaibalini. She is not there.

Nawab. Then, where is she gone?

When *Golston* and *Johnson* were leaving *Pratap's* house, with *Dalani* and *Kulsam*, *Shaibalini* had seen them. She did not know who the women were, and took them to be either maid-servants or dancing girls.

But when the *Nawab's* men told her that the *Begum* was in *Pratap's* house and that she was being taken to the castle in obedience to the Royal command to bring the *Begum*, she at once understood that the Englishmen had taken away with them no other person than the *Begum* herself. *Shaibalini* was thinking what she should say.

"Have you seen the *Begum*?" inquired the *Nawab* impatiently, finding *Shaibalini* silent.

"Yes, I have," was *Shaibalini's* brief reply.

Nawab. Where did you see her?

Shaibalini. At the place where we had been last night.

Nawab. What place is that? Is it *Pratap's* house?

Shaibalini. Yes, if it pleases you.

Nawab. Do you know where the *Begum* has gone?

Shaibalini. Two Englishmen have taken her away.

"What do you say?" inquired the *Nawab* in painful surprise.

Shaibalini repeated what she had said. The *Nawab* was struck dumb in surprise and indignation. He began to bite his lips and pull up his beards in violent agitation. He ordered to summon *Gurgan Khan* before him. He then asked *Shaibalini*,

"Do you know why the Englishmen have taken away the *Begum*?"

Shaibalini. No, I do not.

Nawab. Where was *Pratap* at the time?

Shaibalini. He was in the house, and was also taken away.

Nawab. Was there any one else in the house?

Shaibalini. Yes, there was a servant—he too was taken away.

"Do you know why they were taken away?" again enquired the *Nawab* in an anxious tone.

Hitherto *Shaibalini* was telling the truth; now she began to tell lies. She said, "No."

Nawab. Who is *Pratap Roy*? Where does he come from?

Shaibalini gave *Pratap's* correct designation.

Nawab. What brought him here?

Shaibalini. He came here to enter into the Royal service.

Nawab. What is he to you?

Shaibalini. He is my husband.

Nawab. What is your name?

Shaibalini. My name is *Rupashi*.

Without the slightest difficulty or hesitation, wicked *Shaibalini* made this reply. She had come to the castle to utter this shameful lie.

The *Nawab* said, "I will see what can be done—you better go home now."

Shaibalini. I am now homeless—where shall I go?

The *Nawab* remained silent. After a while he said, "Then, where do you mean to go?"

Shaibalini. To my husband; do please send me to my lord. You are the king, pray listen to my complaint;—the English have taken away my husband by force; either deliver him from their hands or send me to him. If you pay no heed to my prayer and take no steps, I shall put an end to my life here before you.—I have come here with such a purpose.

Just then it was reported to the *Nawab*, that *Gurgan Khan* had come. The *Nawab*, while leaving the room to meet *Gurgan Khan*, said to *Shaibalini*,

"All right, you better wait here—I shall come back presently."

BANKIM CHANDRA CHATTERJEE

III

The New Hobby

The *Nawab*, after making inquiries on several matters, said to *Gurgan Khan*,

"It appears it is in every way desirable that war should be declared against the English. Methinks, *Amyatt* should be arrested before hostilities commence; for he is my pronounced enemy. What do you say to this?"

Gurgan Khan. I am always ready for war; but an envoy should not be severely dealt with. If we oppress him, we shall be guilty of treachery in the eye of the world, and—

"Only last night," interposed the *Nawab* haughtily, "*Amyatt* entered into a house, in this town, by force, and took away the inmates under arrest! Why should I not order the punishment of a man, no matter that he is an envoy, who has committed such a crime within my territories?"

Gurgan Khan. If he has really done so, he is certainly punishable. But how am I to arrest him?

Nawab. Immediately despatch to his quarters some *Sepoys* with a gun, to bring him here with his party, under arrest.

Gurgan Khan. *Amyatt* and his men are not in this town now—they have left it this noon.

Nawab. How is it! Without giving any intimation?

Gurgan Khan. They have left one Mr. Hay for that purpose.

Nawab. What is the reason of their decamping so suddenly, and without my permission? It certainly indicates hostile attitude, and they must have quitted the town with open eyes as to what it would mean.

Gurgan Khan. Last night, some one murdered the English officer in charge of their ammunition boat. *Amyatt* suspects that our men have committed the murder, and has quitted the town in disgust. He is reported to have said that life was not safe here.

Nawab. Have you heard who murdered the man?

Gurgan Khan. Yes, one *Pratap Roy*.

Nawab. Well done! If I meet *Pratap*, I will handsomely reward him. Where is he?

Gurgan Khan. Amyatt has taken away along with him *Pratap* and others. I have, however, received no definite information, whether he has taken them along with him or has sent them to *Azimabad*.

Nawab. Why did you not let me know all these things so long?

Gurgan Khan. I got the informations only a little before.

This was a lie. *Gurgan Khan* knew everything from the very beginning to the end. Without his consent, *Amyatt* could by no means leave *Monghyr*. *Gurgan Khan* had two-fold interest in letting *Amyatt* go. In the first place, he would be safe if *Dalani* was out of *Monghyr*, and secondly, *Amyatt* might do him some good in future if he would oblige him now.

The *Nawab* dismissed *Gurgan Khan*. While he was leaving the place, the *Nawab* cast upon him an askance glance. By that he meant—"So long as the war does not come to an end, I shall not touch a hair of your body— at the time of war you are my best weapon. But after that, I will discharge the debt I owe to *Dalani Begam*, with your blood."

The *Nawab* then summoned before him the *Mir Munshi*, and said, "Issue orders to *Mahammud Taki Khan*, at *Murshidabad*, to arrest *Amyatt* as soon as his boat arrives there, and send the prisoners with him to my court, here. Also, write that the arrest should be skilfully effected without an open engagement. Send a messenger with the order by land—it will then reach *Murshidabad* earlier."

The *Nawab* then returned to the harem, and called in his presence *Shaibalini*, and said, "Your husband cannot be rescued immediately— the Englishmen have left for *Calcutta* with the prisoners. I have sent orders to my officer, at *Murshidabad*, to arrest them there. Now you—"

"Excuse this light woman," interposed *Shaibalini*, with folded hands, "is it not possible to capture them if men are sent now?"

Nawab. It is not possible for a handful of *Sepoys* to arrest the Englishmen. A big boat will be required if a large number of armed men are despatched, and so the rescuing party will not be able to overtake the offenders on this side of *Murshidabad*. Besides, the Englishmen, I am afraid, may put to death all the prisoners, if they notice signs of regular fight. I have clever officers at *Murshidabad*, and they will skilfully effect an arrest.

Shaibalini could feel that her beautiful face has been of great help to her. It must have, she thought, made the *Nawab* believe her every word, and show to her so much kindness; or, why should he care to tell her so many things for her satisfaction? This emboldened *Shaibalini*. She again folded her hands, and said, "If you have been so very kind to this forlorn woman, be pleased to excuse me when I beseech you to listen to another prayer of mine. It is very easy to deliver my husband—he himself is a brave and skilful soldier. If he had weapons in his hand, the Englishmen could not have arrested him, and if he gets arms now, no one will be able to keep him in confinement. If some one can go and give him some weapons, he himself will be able to effect his own release and that of his companions.

The *Nawab* laughed at this, and said, "You are a mere girl and you do not know what sort of people the Englishmen are; who will venture to go upon their boat to give arms to your husband?"

"If you desire it, and if I get a small boat, I myself will go," replied *Shaibalini*, in a low but determined voice, with down-cast eyes.

The *Nawab* laughed aloud. At this, *Shaibalini* contracted her eye-brows, and said with striking firmness, "My lord, if I fail, I shall meet death—that won't affect anybody. But if I be successful, I shall gain my own object and you yours."

The contracted eye-brows of *Shaibalini*, which lent a peculiar grace to her countenance, convinced the *Nawab* that she was not an ordinary woman. He thought within himself, "Let her go. If she succeeds so much the better, if not, *Mahammud Taki* will accomplish the object, at *Murshidabad*." He then said to *Shaibalini*, "Would you go alone?"

"I am a woman, I shall not be able to go alone. If you will be so kind to me, please order a maid-servant and an armed man to accompany me," replied *Shaibalini* entreatingly.

The *Nawab* remained silent for a while, and then ordered to call in his presence *Mashibuddin*, a faithful, strong and courageous eunoch attendant. The man came there, and made his obeisance to his Royal master. The *Nawab* said to him, "Immediately set out, with this lady, in a small boat, for *Murshidabad*. Take along with you some arms, which she may select, and a *Hindu* maid-servant."

"What duty shall I have to perform at *Murshidabad*?" inquired *Mashibuddin* respectfully.

"You shall do what she will command," replied the *Nawab*, "Honour her as a *Begum*. If you meet *Dalani Begum*, bring her along with you."

After this, they both saluted the *Nawab* in the proper form, and took leave of him. *Shaibalini* imitated the eunoch attendant in his observance of the court etiquette. Like him, she receded from the *Nawab* without showing her back and repeatedly saluted him, as she withdrew herself, touching the floor with her hands. The *Nawab* smiled at this, and said,

"Remember me, fair lady. If you are ever in difficulty, come to *Mir Kashim* for help."

At this, *Shaibalini* made a profound bow to the *Nawab*. She said within herself, "Of course, I shall—I shall perhaps, come to you for the settlement of my dispute with *Rupashi*, in respect of *Pratap*."

Mashibuddin got a maid-servant and a boat ready, and at the instance of *Shaibalini*, procured swords, daggers, guns, revolvers, bullets and powder. He did not venture to ask *Shaibalini* as to what she would do with them. He thought within himself that she was another *Chand Sultana*.

They got into the boat, and set out that very night.

IV

She Weeps

The glorious moon was then smiling upon the world. On both sides of the flowing *Bhagirathi*, there were wide expanses of sands, which in the radiance of the moonlight wore a brighter and a more charming silvery beauty; the blue water of the *Ganges* were flashed with a brighter blue, in the brilliancy of that light. So was the sky over-head, with its sparkling jewels, and the trees on the bank, with their evergreen mantles. There was blue all around. In such moments, the thought of the vastness of the universe agitates the mind. The flow of the river knows no end; it has no limit so far as the eye can see—like the human fate it disappears in the misty womb of the unknown. The river was unlimited, so were the sands around, the trees on the banks, and the sky above, with its numberless starry garlands. In the face of such vastness, what man on earth can count himself as a unit of this stupendous and wonderful creation of God? Where would the pride of man be in the presence of such an all-pervading majesty, which was, in that solemn moment, manifested even in a particle of sand, lying on the river shore?

At a place by the river shore, there lay fastened a row of boats, one of which was a big *Budgrow*. On it, there were sentinels on watch. The two guards, stood firm and motionless, with their guns on their shoulders, like two statues of stone. Within the boat, beautiful varieties of costly chairs, sofas, pictures and statues and many other furnitures were glittering in the soft light of a valuable lamp, made of highly perfect glass. There were some Englishmen within the cabin. Two of them were playing at chess, one was drinking wine in poring over a book, and the other was playing on a musical instrument.

All on a sudden, they got startled at the fearful wail of lamentation, which rose from the river shore, disturbing the stillness of night.

"What's that?" inquired *Amyatt*, as he offered a check to his opponent's king.

"Some one, perhaps, has been checkmated," replied *Johnson* wittily.

The wails grew more fearful. The sound itself was not hideous or horrible, but in the night, in that wide lonely river shore, it resounded like a dreadful cry.

Amyatt gave up playing, and rose up. He came out of the cabin, and began to look around. He saw nobody. He noticed that there was no burning-place near by, and the sound was coming from the middle of the sandy bank. *Amyatt* then alighted from the boat and followed up the sound. After he had advanced a little, he saw some one sitting alone on the sands. He drew nearer, and found that a woman was crying aloud. He did not know *Hindi* Well, but nevertheless asked the woman, "Who are you? Why are you crying here?" The woman could not understand his wonderful *Hindi*, and continued to cry aloud, as before.

Amyatt not having received any reply to his repeated queries, made a sign to her to follow him. The woman rose up at the hint. *Amyatt* moved on, and she followed him, crying all the way as before. She was no other than wicked *Shaibalini* herself.

V

She Laughs

Amyatt returned to the *Budgrow*, and said to *Golston*, "This woman was weeping by the river-side, alone. She does not understand me nor do I her. You better enquire what is the matter with her."

Golston, after all, was almost as clever in *Hindi* as *Amyatt*; but among his own fellows, he was suffered to pass for an expert. He asked the woman,

"Who are you?"

Shaibalini made no answer. She continued to weep.

Golston. "Why are you weeping?"

Yet *Shaibalini* gave no reply, and wept on.

Golston. "Where do you live?"

Shaibalini kept on as before.

Golston. "What has brought you here?"

Shaibalini remained silent, weeping as before.

Golston was at his wit's end. The Englishmen got no answer from *Shaibalini*, and asked her to go away. *Shaibalini*, however, did not seem to understand that—she did not stir—she stood there, as before.

Amyatt then said, "She does not understand us and we do not understand her too. From her dress it appears that she is a *Bengalee* girl. Just call here a *Bengalee* and ask him to question her."

Almost all the attendants of these Englishmen were *Bengalee Mahomedans*. *Amyatt* called one of them in his presence, and asked him to speak to her.

"Why do you weep?" inquired the servant.

Shaibalini burst into laughter, as if, she was mad.

"Sirs, she is a mad woman," said the servant to his masters.

"Ask her what she wants," said the Englishmen out of curiosity.

On being asked, *Shaibalini* said that she was hungry, and the servant explained this to his masters.

"Give her something to eat," enjoined *Amyatt* on his servant.

The menial took her away to the kitchen, with a delightful heart—delightful, because *Shaibalini* was exceedingly handsome. But *Shaibalini* did not eat anything, inspite of the entreaties of the servant. She said to him, "I am a *Brahmin's* daughter; why should I take food from your hands?"

The servant left and reported to his masters what *Shaibalini* had said.

"Is there no *Brahmin* in any of the boats?" inquired *Amyatt* of the servant.

"There is one *Brahmin* among the *Sepoys* and another among the prisoners," replied the man.

"If there is rice with any one of them, go and ask him to give some to the woman," said *Amyatt* in good grace.

The servant, thereupon, took *Shaibalini* to the *Hindu Sepoy*. But he had nothing to give her to eat. The servant, therefore, brought *Shaibalini* to the boat, in which the *Brahmin* prisoner was kept. The prisoner was none but *Pratap Roy* himself.

Pratap was alone in a small boat. Both at its front and back, there were sentinels on watch. There was no light within the boat.

The servant called out the prisoner, and said, "Have you any rice left with you?"

"What will you do with it?" inquired *Pratap*.

"A *Brahmin* girl has had no meals yet—can you give her some rice?" said the servant.

Pratap too had no rice with him. But he did not say so—he said, "yes I can—but ask the sentinel to take off my handcuff."

The servant, thereupon, asked the sentinel to take off *Pratap's* handcuff. But the guard refused to do so without orders. The servant, therefore, went to *Amyatt* to obtain his permission.

Who takes so much trouble for a stranger? Particularly, so much attention could not be expected of *Pirbuksh*; for he drew his pay from an English master, and was never in the habit of helping any one willingly. Of all classes of men in the world, the *Mahomedan* servants of Anglo-Indians are the worst. But *Pirbuksh* had some interest in doing this little service for *Shaibalini*. He thought within himself that he would take the woman to the servants' quarter after she had taken some food, and so he became anxious to win over her by serving her with a meal. He, therefore, left to obtain *Amyatt's* orders—*Shaibalini* meanwhile waited outside *Pratap's* boat, drawing a veil over her face.

A beautiful face achieves triumphs everywhere. Particularly, if a young woman happens to be the possessor of a beautiful face, its influence becomes irresistible. *Amyatt* had seen that the woman was a matchless beauty—he was also somewhat moved to find that she was

BANKIM CHANDRA CHATTERJEE

mad. He, therefore, sent orders through the head of the sentinels, to take off *Pratap's* handcuff, and allow *Shaibalini* to go within the boat.

Pirbuksh brought a light, and the sentry took off *Pratap's* handcuff. *Pratap* took the light, from the servant, and asked him not to come upon the boat. He then went inside with the light, and pretended, as if, he was getting rice for the woman—his object was to escape. *Shaibalini* too came within the boat. The sentinels were keeping watch outside— they could not see what was going on within the boat. *Shaibalini* drew up her veil, and took her seat before *Pratap*.

When *Pratap* got over his surprise, he noticed that *Shaibalini* was biting her lips—her face was rather bright with joy, and bore signs of unswerving determination. *Pratap* felt that *Shaibalini* was in every way fit to be the heroine of a hero like himself.

"Take off your hand from the pot and wash it—am I a beggar for rice?" whispered *Shaibalini* into *Pratap's* ears.

Pratap washed his hand readily.

"Now quit this place in all haste. Know it that the small boat, you will find after that yonder bend of the river, is meant for you," again whispered *Shaibalini* to *Pratap*.

"You go first or you will not be safe," said *Pratap* in a very low whispering voice.

"Away—be gone forthwith," urged *Shaibalini* with all the emphasis she could command. "You won't be able to escape if you are handcuffed again. Jump into the water at once. Don't delay. Be guided by me for a day at least. I shall jump into the water like a mad woman, and you will follow me, as if, to my rescue."

Shaibalini then rose up. She burst into a shrill unnatural laughter, and cried out, "I shall not eat rice." Immediately after this, she began to weep, and said, as she came out of the boat, "I have been fed with a *Mahomedan's* rice—I have lost my caste—Mother *Ganges*, give me shelter in your sacred bosom." *Shaibalini* then threw herself into the river.

Pratap came out of the boat instantly, as if, in great surprise. The sentinel was going to stop him, when he kicked down the man, saying, "Rascal, a woman is about to drown herself in your presence, and you are standing here quite indifferent!"

At that single kick, the sentry fell down from the boat, on the bank. *Pratap* then leaped into the water, crying out, "To the rescue—to the rescue of the dying woman."

Shaibalini, who was an expert in swimming, was going ahead, and *Pratap* was following her.

The sentinel at the back of the boat then raised a hue and cry, and levelled his gun at *Pratap*. *Pratap* saw this, and cried out to the man, "Don't be afraid—I don't mean to get away—I will save that woman—how can I suffer my heart to see her perish for want of help. You are a *Hindu*—don't sin by killing a *Brahmin* for nothing."

The *Sepoy* lowered his gun.

At that time, *Shaibalini* was swimming away by the side of the last boat in the row. At the very sight of it she got startled. She saw that it was the very *Bundgerow* in which she had to live with *Foster*. She fixed her eyes on the boat for a while, and began to tremble with fear. She saw, in the moonlight, on the top of the boat, an Englishman, lying on a little sofa, in a half reclining state. The radiant beams of the moon had fallen upon his face. *Shaibalini* shrieked out when she found that the man on the sofa was no other than *Lawrence Foster* himself!

Lawrence Foster was also gazing at her, as she was swimming away, and recognised that it was *Shaibalini*. He forthwith cried out, "Seize, ho, seize my lady there!" *Foster* himself was sick and bed rid—he had not the power to get up.

At *Foster's* cry, four or five men jumped into the river to seize *Shaibalini*. *Pratap* was at that time far ahead of them. They cried out to him, "Seize that woman—*Foster Sahib* will reward you. At this, *Pratap* said within himself, "I myself once gave *Foster* some reward, and I have a mind to reward him again." He, however, shouted to the men, "I will seize her—you better go back."

The men relied on *Pratap's* words, and turned back. *Foster* could not recognise that the man in advance was *Pratap* himself. Even then *Foster's* brain was not thoroughly restored.

VI

Along Deep Waters

Pratap and *Shaibalini* now came to at a great distance. What a charming sight it was! What a pleasant journey it was for them, through that sea of happiness! Their eyes fell upon the beauties of the deep blue vault of the sky overhead, as they floated away on the wide and wavy stream of the *Bhagirathi*, now flashed with the silvery hue of the shining moon, flowing incessantly through innumerable countries, for endless time. At the sight of this grand spectacle, *Pratap* thought within himself, "Alas! why is not man privileged to glide through the deep bosom of that yonder sea above? Why is not man able to break through those waves of clouds? What pious deed can achieve for me a life which is privileged to swim in that sea? To swim?—What a trifle it is to swim in these earthly rivers! Since the day of my birth, I have been swimming in the ruffled sea of life—pushing waves upon waves, and being myself tossed about by them, like a straw. After this, who would care to swim in the rivers of this world?" *Shaibalini* thought that the river she was swimming in had a bottom, but the sea of her trouble was unfathomable!

Whether you care for the, beauties of nature or not, they will not let you go unmoved and unimpressed by their charms—beauties never pass unnoticed. It does not matter in what sea you may happen to swim, the beauty of the blue water does not lose its charms—the string of wavelets is not torn—the stars overhead shine with usual brilliancy—the trees on the bank wave and swing as before, and the shooting beams of the moon play on the water as usual. Such is the beautiful tyranny of Nature! Like an affectionate mother she is always anxious to fondle and caress.

All these *Pratap* could see, but *Shaibalini's* eyes were blind to them. The pale and emaciated white face which she had seen on the top of the *Budgerow*, exclusively occupied her mind, and she was swimming but mechanically. But there was no rest—both of them were experts in swimming. *Pratap* was taking great delight in swimming along the placid waters of the flowing *Bhagirathi*—his heart was simply overflowing with joy. He called out in an affectionate and cheerful voice,

"Shaibalini—Shai!"

This warm and loving address thrilled *Shaibalini* through and through—her heart beat violently within her. In their younger days, *Pratap* took delight in calling her, "*Shai*" or "*Sai*," and it was after a long, long time that he again addressed her in that sweet familiar mode! The fleeting away of time cannot be measured by months or years. Its flow is swift or tardy as our situation is pleasant or unpleasant. To *Shaibalini*, the few days she had not been greeted by *Pratap* in that fond and affectionate manner, appeared to be as long as the great interval between two ages. *Shaibalini* was overpowered with emotion, and she closed her eyes, as she was gliding away through that vast sheet of water; she asked the moon and the stars over her head, to bear witness to what had fallen from *Pratap's* lips. She then said, with her eyes closed as before,

"*Pratap*, why even to day the silvery beams of the moon should smile upon the waters of the Ganges?"

Pratap. *Shai!* We are safe now—no one is pursuing us.

Shaibalini. Let us then get up on the bank.

Pratap. *Shai!*

Shaibalini. What will you say, *Pratap*?

Pratap. Do you still remember?

Shaibalini. What is it, *Pratap*?

Pratap. Do you remember that never-to-be-forgotten-day, when we both swam in the river as we do now?

Shaibalini made no answer. A large piece of wood was floating away close to them; *Shaibalini* caught hold of it, and said to *Pratap*,

"Hold it—it shall bear your weight. Take some rest."

Pratap did so, and said, "Do you remember that on that occasion I sank into the water to drown myself, but you could not?"

"Yes I do," replied *Shaibalini*. "But if you had not again addressed me in that fond affectionate manner, I would have here paid off the debt I owe you. Why have you revived in me the happy memories of a pleasant past by your affectionate call?"

Pratap. Then, you know that I can drown myself here, if I like?

"Why, *Pratap*? Let us get up on the bank," said *Shaibalini* in great anxiety.

Pratap. I won't get up—I will die here.

Pratap left the support.

Shaibalini. Why do you say so, *Pratap*?

Pratap. It is no joke—I will surely drown myself here. Let me have your hand.

Shaibalini. What do you want of me, *Pratap*? I will do anything you like, for your sake.

Pratap. First make a promise to me, and then I shall get up.

Shaibalini too now left the support. In her eyes, the stars ceased to shine, the moon grew pale and sickly, and the blue water of the river seemed to blaze like blue fire. She saw, as if *Foster* had come and stood before her in a threatening attitude, with a sword in hand. *Pratap* and *Shaibalini* were swimming side by side, close to each other. The heart-rending conversation between them was going on in the midst of the pattering noise of the breaking ripples. The smiling image of the glorious moon could then be seen most charmingly reflected in the fine particles of water which were shooting up in silvery fountains on all sides. This again, was the beautiful tyranny of Nature! *Shaibalini*, who could not speak for a time, at last said, almost suffocated under the pressure of a painful anxiety,

"What promise, *Pratap*?"

Pratap. Promise on the sacred waters of the *Ganges*—

Shaibalini. What right has a sinner like me to swear in the name of the holy *Ganges*?

Pratap. Then swear in the name of Religion—

Shaibalini. Ah, I have fallen from it long ago.

Pratap. Will you then swear by me?

Shaibalini. Come nearer, and let me have your hand.

Pratap came closer to *Shaibalini*, and took her hand in his, after a long, long time. It then became very difficult for them to swim. They again caught hold of the support.

Shaibalini then said, "Now I am ready to swear anything you like. *Pratap*, after what a long time I clasp your hand in mine!"

Pratap. Swear by me, or I will drown myself here. What is this life for? Who will willingly bear the burden of a sinful life? What can be more desirable than to lay down that burden on the sacred bosom of the flowing *Bhagirathi*, under the silvery radiance of the glorious moon?

The moon was then smiling overhead.

Shaibalini. I swear by you—tell me what I am to do.

Pratap. Swear—swear by me—that you shall be responsible for my weal and woe, yea, for my life and death.

Shaibalini. Yes, in your name I promise that throughout my life I will unswervingly act up to your wishes.

Pratap then demanded a most painful promise. To *Shaibalini* it was very cruel and severe—its fulfilment was beyond her powers, yea, it meant her death. She recoiled from it, and said,

"*Pratap*, is there a second person in this world who is as miserable as myself?"

Pratap. It is me, *Shaibalini*!

Shaibalini. You have wealth—you have strength—you have ambition—you have fame—you have friends and then you have *Rupashi*. What have I as my own, *Pratap*?

Pratap. Nothing—then come, let us both drown ourselves here.

Shaibalini reflected for a moment. As the result of her thought, the current of her life began to run, for the first time, in the opposite direction. She thought within herself, "What harm is there if I die? But, why should *Pratap* die for me?" She then said to *Pratap*,

"Let us get up on the bank."

Pratap left the support, and sank into the water. Even then *Pratap's* hand was in *Shaibalini's* clasp. She pulled *Pratap* by his hand, and he got up. *Shaibalini* then said,

"*Pratap*, I will swear. But just think for a moment, you are going to deprive me of all that I have in this world. I don't want you, but why should I give up your thought?"

Pratap took away his hand, but *Shaibalini* grasped it again. Then in a deep sombre voice, clear and distinct, although affected by emotions, *Shaibalini* began to speak. She said,

"*Pratap*, clasp my hand firmly. Listen, I swear by you that I am responsible for your life and death. In your name I promise that I shall not think of you henceforth. I shall sacrifice all my happiness to control my mind. From this day, *Shaibalini* will be dead, though alive."

Shaibalini took away her hand from *Pratap's* clasp, and also left the support. *Pratap* then said to her, in a voice of deep emotion,

"*Shaibalini*, let us now get up on the bank."

They both got up. Walking up a little distance, they took a turn at the bend of the river. The little boat which *Shaibalini* had brought with her from the *Nawab*, was not far off. They both got up on it, and set out forthwith. Neither of them could see that *Ramananda Swami* was observing them very closely.

Shaibalini lost her suit against *Rupashi*, even before she could file her plaint in the royal court of the *Nawab*.

VII

RAMCHARAN RELEASED

When *Pratap* made his escape, *Ramcharan* effected his release very easily. He was not living as a prisoner. Nobody knew that it was his shots which had wounded *Foster* and killed the sentry, on the night *Shaibalini* was rescued from *Foster's Budgerow. Amyatt* had taken him to be a common servant and was quite willing to let him off while he was leaving *Monghyr.* He told *Ramcharan* at that time, "Your master is a great rogue—we will punish him severely; but we have nothing to do with you—you may go wherever you like." At this *Ramcharan* saluted *Amyatt*, and said with folded hands, "I am a rustic peasant—I don't know manners—pray don't take offence at my words—do you bear any relation to me?"

Some one in the boat explained to *Amyatt* what *Ramcharan* had said. Thereupon *Amyatt* asked,

"Why—what makes you say so?"

Ramcharan. If it is not so, how is it that you are joking with me?

Amyatt. What joke do you mean?

Ramcharan. Is it not a joke to ask me to go away anywhere I like, after breaking my leg? It shows that I have married in your family—I am a *Hindu* milkman's son, I shall lose my caste if I marry an Englishman's sister.

Notwithstanding the explanation of the interpreter, *Amyatt* could not make a head or tail of what *Ramcharan* had said. He thought within himself that it was a kind of Indian flattery. He concluded that as "natives" in flattering Englishmen, called them "Father," "Mother," or "Brother," so *Ramcharan* was addressing him as his *brother-in-law* only to please him. He was rather not displeased with *Ramcharan*, and asked,

"What do you want?"

"Pray, order to set right my broken leg," replied *Ramcharan* with a fine cunningness.

"All right, you better stay with us for some time—I will give you some medicine," said *Amyatt* with a smile.

That was exactly what *Ramcharan* wanted. *Pratap* was then being taken away as a prisoner, and it was *Ramcharan's* earnest desire to be with him. For this reason, he of his own accord had accompanied *Amyatt*. He, however, had not to live as a prisoner.

On the very night, *Pratap* made his escape, *Ramcharan* alighted from the boat without speaking to anybody, and stealthily left the place. He abused, in an inaudible voice, the English people, to his heart's content, as he went away. His leg had become all right again.

VIII

On the Hills

The moon did not appear that night to smile upon the world below. Dark clouds had covered the sky, the moon, the stars and all the lesser luminaries. The clouds which were full of rains, and were therefore tinged dark gray, had all gathered together into a thick unbroken mass, which enveloped the whole firmament—made it an all pervading endless expanse of impenetrable darkness, which covered the river, its sandy banks, and the land above, with the chain of hills on it. In that darkness *Shaibalini* was alone in the valley of the hills.

In the latter part of the night the little boat, in which *Pratap* and *Shaibalini* made their escape, was taken to the shore, keeping the pursuing enemies at a distance. There is no dearth of retired places by the side of large rivers, and the little boat was fastened to one of such secluded nooks. There *Shaibalini* left the boat, unnoticed. This time, she did not run away for any evil purpose. It is that fear of life which drives away the animals of a burning forest, prompted her to desert *Pratap's* company. It was only for fear of life that *Shaibalini* resolved to forsake society with all its joys and pleasures. She had no longer any claim to happiness, love and friendship, or even to her most beloved *Pratap*. She had no hope for all these things—even the very desire of obtaining them in life was to be abandoned. Who can give up the desire and yet be with the object of craving? What thirsty traveller, in a bleak desert, can pass on, with parched lips, without drinking from the pure transparent water, he comes across in his way? Rapacious greed and inordinate desire, in respect of their influences on human mind, can be rightly compared with the dreadful and all-devouring sea-devil, as described by *Victor-Hugo*. This horrible animal lives in water which equals even crystals in transparency, and where stones of different colours and varieties sparkle and glow with a lustre all their own; innumerable priceless pearls and corals also illumine the beautiful habitation of this dreadful monster. It is dreadful because it sucks human blood. The unfortunate man who goes near it, being fascinated by the beautiful sight of its home, is caught hold of by this devil, who stretches out its awful hundred hands one by one, to grasp its victim in its clutches, so tight as to render all rescue impossible. The monster, thus securing the prey in its grip, begins to suck its life-blood.

Shaibalini, finding herself unfit for the struggle, took to heels. She had this fear in her mind that *Pratap* would try to find her out as soon as he would come to know that she had escaped. For this reason, she had gone as far as she could, without halting anywhere in the way. She could see before her, at no great distance, that chain of hills which can appropriately be called the belt of *Hindusthan*. She did not mount the hills during the day, lest any one of the searching party would discover her. She hid herself somewhere in the forest, and passed the whole day without any food. Slowly and gradually the twilight of the evening faded away, and darkness covered the face of the earth. The moon was to appear that night long after the sunset. *Shaibalini* began to ascend the hills in darkness. She got many wounds in her feet, as she made her way through the thorny plants and stones, lying scattered on the hills; it was not possible to find out a smooth track in the midst of the rank growth of little shrubs and creepers. Her hands too were bleeding at the thorns and pricks of those wild plants, the sharp pointed ends of broken boughs and the stump of trees. Now commenced *Shaibalini's* penance. All these, however, did not cause pain and suffering to *Shaibalini*. She had made up her mind to undergo that penance. Willingly and of her own accord, she had deserted the blissful society, and entered into that dreadful wilderness of the hills, full of wild and ferocious beasts. So long she lay immersed in the dark and endless abyss of sin, and would not the burden of her crime be lightened if she would now undergo the penance by calmly bearing the inflictions of pain and suffering? So *Shaibalini*, sick with thirst and hunger—her body bleeding all over—began to ascend the hills without any rest. No beaten track could be seen—the falling shade of night had then covered everything with darkness. But then, even during the day it was not possible to trace out a way of easy access in the midst of the overgrowing shrubs and innumerable stones of those hills. *Shaibalini*, therefore,

"She took her seat in a thorny bush, in utter despair."

could ascend but very little, and even that with great difficulty.

Just then, dark clouds were seen to gather overhead, and the sky soon became overcast with them. It seemed, as if, the vault of heaven had been enveloped by a black imperforated screen. Darkness of endless volume, growing thicker and thicker every moment, descended from above to the world below, and gradually covered the hills, the road beneath, the distant river, and, in fact, all the surrounding objects of nature. The whole universe, it seemed, was nothing but an endless mass of impenetrable darkness—to *Shaibalini* it appeared that in this world there was nothing but stones, thorns and darkness. She felt that it was useless to try to ascend higher up, and so she took her seat in a thorny bush, in utter despair. Just then, quick flashes and streaks of lightning were seen to run their serpentine course from one end of the firmament to the other. With them commenced the deafening claps of thunder. It was a horrible sight! *Shaibalini* could understand that all these were the signs of a severe summer storm which would soon burst forth in that mountainous region. What harm was there in that? Many a tree and bough, many a leaf and flower, would be torn away from the hills and destroyed—would it not end so happily with *Shaibalini*?

All on a sudden, *Shaibalini* perceived the touch of some cold substance on her body. It was a drop of rain. Another drop—still another—then drop after drop began to fall in quicker succession till at last they fell in copious showers. Then followed a horrible noise that filled the air all around. It was a confused mixture of sounds which emanated from the pattering rains, the howling gust and the roaring thunder clouds; with it were heard, at times, the clamour of falling boughs, the wails of frightened beasts, the rumbling noise of shifted stones, rolling down the slopes of the hills, and the bustle and commotion of the tumultous waves of the distant *Bhagirathi*, wrestling with one another with mad enthusiasm. *Shaibalini* was seated on the hill, upon a stone, with her head bent down—the cold drops of rain were being incesssantly showered upon it. The boughs of small trees and the little branches of shrubs and creepers, which were waving to and fro in the strong gale, began to strike her body repeatedly, in their alternate rise and fall. The torrents of rain water, from the mountain top, was rushing down the slope of the hill in streams, covering *Shaibalini* up to her thigh.

Nature, Thou all-powerful mistress of the dead elements, before Thee humanity must fall prostrate to pay its tribute of homage and admiration! Thou hast no mercy, no love, no affection in Thee—Thou shrinkest not to destroy life—Thou art the parent of endless misery, yet the world is indebted to Thee for what it is; for Thou art at the same time the fountain head of all joy and happiness, the dispenser of all blessings, the distributer of weal and the fulfiller of all hopes and aspirations—Thou art perfect! Before Thee, therefore, the world must bow down in veneration. Oh, Thou dreadful, or what Thou art we know not! only last night Thou hadst appeared before the world with a glorious moon shining on Thy forehead and a superb crown of the sparkling stars, adorning Thy head, and moved the universe with thy all-captivating smile; Thou hadst knitted a beautiful wreath with the waving ripples of the flowing *Bhagirathi*, and hadst suspended against each of them a moon; again, Thou hadst given the brilliancy of diamonds to each particle of sand, on the river shore, and made the youthful pair happy, by floating them in the blue bosom of the Ganges! It seemed Thou wert very kind and loving; for how sweetly Thou hadst fondled and caressed them. But what is this today? Thou art untrustworthy and all-destroying. We do not know why Thou makest animals Thy sport—Thou hast no wisdom, no knowledge, no life, no sensation, yet Thou art omnipresent, omnipotent and all destroying—Thou art the magic-illusion of God, the brightest manifestation of His glory—Thou art really unconquerable. Humanity must bow down before Thy Majesty.

The rain ceased after a long time, but the storm was still raging; only its fury had abated a little. The all-encompassing darkness had now become denser than before. *Shaibalini* could feel that it was not possible for her to ascend or descend the slippery hills in that ungodly hour, and so she remained seated there, shivering with cold. Her once dear home at *Bedagram*, now came into her recollections. She thought within herself, "I would die happier if I could once again see that abode of peace and happiness. But not to speak of that, I would not, perhaps, live to see even the light of the morning. Death, whose aid I had so long vainly invoked, is upon me today."

Just then, on that desolate hill, within that inaccessible thicket, in that unearthly period of impenetrable darkness, some one touched *Shaibalini's* body. At first she thought it was some beast of the forest; so she moved away a little. But again she perceived that touch on her body, and this time she could distinctly feel that it was exactly the touch of a human hand—nothing, however, could be seen in the darkness. *Shaibalini* then in a fear-stricken voice asked, "Who are you? Are you an angel or a man?" *Shaibalini* had no reason to be afraid of man, but she could not but dread the Gods; for they are the dispensers of justice.

Nobody gave any answer to *Shaibalini's* query. But she could feel, be it a man or an angel, she was being grasped by somebody. She found that a hand was placed on her back and another clasped her legs, and that she was being lifted up. At this, she burst forth into a scream. After a while, she could perceive that she was being carried somewhere, and that her carrier was ascending the hills very carefully with her. *Shaibalini* thought that whoever he may be, he was certainly not *Lawrence Foster*.

PART IV
THE PENANCE

I

What Pratap Did

P ratap was a *Zemindar* and a plunderer too. At the time of which we are speaking, almost all the *Zemindars* of this country were plunderers. *Darwin* has said that man has sprung originally from the monkey tribe. If people do not take offence or get annoyed at this theory, we may, perhaps, reasonably hope that no *Zemindar* of the present generation will be displeased with us for our remarks regarding their ancestry. To speak the truth, it does not seem to be in any way dishonourable or inglorious for a man to have descended from an ancient stock of plunderers; for elsewhere we find that many people of such a lineage occupy the highest position in society, so far as family prestige is concerned. The descendants of the famous plunderer, *Timour*, had risen to the highest social eminence in the whole world. In England, those who desire to indulge in family pride call themselves descendants of the Norman or the Scandinavian sea-robbers. In ancient India, the *Kouravas* enjoyed the highest social rank and status, and they were but plunderers—they had attempted to rob King *Birat's* cows. There are only a very few *Zemindar* families in Bengal who have to some extent such family reputation.

But then, *Pratap* was not exactly a plunderer of the type of the ancient *Zemindars*. He sought and employed the services of robbers and plunderers, only when it was necessary either for the security of his own property or for the submission of a wicked and unyielding enemy. He did so, not to rob people of their properties or to unnecessarily oppress them, but, in fact, only to protect the feeble and the oppressed. *Pratap* was now about to have recourse to such means once again.

On the morning of the very night *Shaibalini* stole away from the boat, *Pratap* was delighted to find that *Ramcharan* had come there; but he became anxious for not finding *Shaibalini* in the boat. He waited for her a while, and when she did not turn up, he began to search for her. He made a search on the bank of the river till the day had far advanced, but did not find her. In despair, *Pratap* concluded that *Shaibalini* must have drowned herself in the river. He could feel that it was no longer impossible for her to commit suicide in that way.

Pratap at first thought that he was the cause of *Shaibalini's* death, but he also felt that he had never deviated from the path of virtue and trodden on that of sin, and the cause for which *Shaibalini* had put an end to her life was more than what he could remove. So *Pratap* did not find any reason to blame himself. He blamed *Chandra Shekhar* a little for having married *Shaibalini*. Again, he became a little angry with *Rupashi*—why had she been married to him instead of *Shaibalini*? He became a bit more angry with *Sundari*; for if she had not set *Pratap* to *Shaibalini's* rescue, he would have had no occasion to swim with her along the waters of the Ganges, and so she would not have died. But *Pratap* became most angry with *Foster*; for if he had not caused *Shaibalini* to desert her husband's home, all this would not have happened at all. Then again, if the English had not come out to India, *Shaibalini* would not have fallen into *Foster's* hands, and so an irresistible feeling of hatred for the English sprang up in *Pratap's* mind. *Pratap* decided that he would again get hold of *Foster*, and put an end to his sinful life. This time, he would burn into ashes *Foster's* dead body, or he would again escape death—if he would bury him he might rend his way out of the grave. He also decided that it was highly desirable to drive the English "out" of Bengal; for there might be many more *Fosters* among them.

Pratap returned to *Monghyr* in that small boat, meditating all the way. He entered into the Castle and found that preparations for war against the English were being made there with ardent zeal and enthusiasm. *Pratap* was much gratified at this. He thought within himself, "Will not the *Nawab* be able to drive the devils out of Bengal? Would not *Foster* be seized? It is the duty of every man to help the *Nawab* in this matter, to the extent of his capacity. Even the squirrels could bridge up the sea, can I not render any assistance? What can I do? I have no trained soldiers—I have only *Lathials* and gangs of plunderers at my beck and call; can they be of any service? The work of pillage, if not anything else, can be carried on with them. With their help I shall be able to plunder any village that will render help to the English. Wherever I shall find provisions of the enemies, I shall plunder them. I shall take to pillaging whenever I shall find their transport in course of being taken from one place to another. In this way I shall be able to do the *Nawab* much good. The victory in an open engagement is but an ordinary means of destroying the enemies. To barricade the enemy at their back and to obstruct them in their attempts to collect provisions are the principal expedients to ensure success in war. I shall do all that lies in my power so far as these two stratagems are concerned. But then, why should I do so much? There are many reasons for it. In the first place the English have brought about *Chandra Shekhar's* complete ruin; secondly *Shaibalini* has met death on their account; thirdly they had imprisoned me; and lastly they have done and are still doing such mischief to others. I shall, therefore, give effect to my designs against them.

Pratap won over the leading officials of the *Nawab* by flattery, and through them obtained an interview with the *Nawab*. What talk he had with the *Nawab*, no one came to know. After the interview *Pratap* left for his own native village.

Rupashi was relieved of her anxiety for *Pratap*, on his return home, after a long time. But she was much mortified at the news of *Shaibalini's* death. *Sundari* came to see *Pratap* when she heard he had come back. She was extremely grieved to hear that *Shaibalini* was no more. But she said, "*Shaibalini* has now become happy. How can I have the front to deny that, for her, death was by all means better than life?"

Pratap again left home. Soon after his departure, the news widely spread throughout the length and breadth of the country that *Pratap Roy* had been collecting together all the plunderers and *Lathials* of the places between *Monghyr* and *Cutwa*.

II

What Shaibalini Did

In a dark cave, *Shaibalini* was lying on a prickly bed of stones. The stalwart man, who had come to her rescue, while she was being exposed to the severe storm, on the hills, left her in that den of impenetrable darkness. The storm and rain ceased, but within the cave there was darkness and nothing but darkness, which was rendered more hideous by the deadly silence that prevailed there. Yea, so dark was the cell, where *Shaibalini* was cast by the cruel tyranny of fate, that it made the vision of man as terribly obscure as when the eyes are closed. There was nothing to disturb the stillness of death which reigned in that fearful place except the occasional pattering sounds of water, falling in drops on the stones, through the cracks and crevices above the cave. Besides, the breath of some animal, who knows whether it was a man or a beast, could be perceived in that abode of horrible solitude and darkness.

It was now for the first time that fear seized *Shaibalini*. Was it fear? No, not exactly that. The range of human intellect, in a state of equilibrium, has well defined limits—poor *Shaibalini* had gone beyond that. She had nothing on earth to be afraid of; for her life had become an unbearable burden, and she felt that the sooner she could lay it down the better for her. All she could prize besides life, such as happiness, virtue, honour, caste and family distinction, she had already lost. What else had she to lose? How could fear be possible at such a stage of life? On that day, or perhaps before, *Shaibalini* had banished from her heart the fond hope which she had, from the very early years of her life, secretly fostered, with tender care—she had abandoned her most dear thing on earth for which she had willingly sacrificed all the pleasures and happiness of this world. After this, it was quite natural that her mind became deranged and lost all its strength and energy. Her body too was enfeebled; for she had no food for two days, and the fatigue and exhaustion caused in ascending the hills, through a thorny and inaccessible path, during a severe storm, had proved simply trying. Then again, the mysterious way in which *Shaibalini* was carried on the top of the hill and thrown into that dismal cave, with all its horrible associations—a fearful incident which at least *Shaibalini* thought to have been brought about by the agency of supernatural beings—produced a terrible effect on her mind. All those things combined to unnerve and break down *Shaibalini*—what more could human constitution endure? *Shaibalini* was lying in that bed of stones in an almost unconscious state. She was neither asleep nor awake—a cold morbid stupor had dulled both her mind and body. Gradually she lost all her senses. She then saw, in a vision, the endless course of a flowing river. But it seemed to her that the river had no water in it—it was a current of blood that overflowed the banks. She saw in it rotten human bodies, skulls and skeletons, floating away in a hideous manner. Dreadful animals, resembling huge crocodiles in their shape and form, devoid of flesh and skin, with only their skeleton intact and eyes flashing fire, were seen to move here and there, devouring the rotten bodies. She felt that the stalwart man, who had carried her to that hideous cave, now brought her to the bank of that fearful river. It seemed that in that horrible region, there was no sun, no moon, no star, no light, yet there was nothing like darkness. Every object there could be seen, though very faintly. The river of blood, the rotten human bodies, the floating bones, the fearful crocodiles in mere skeleton, all these could be seen, although there was no light. On the banks, instead of sands there were sharp pins, with their pointed ends upwards. The colossal figure of *Shaibalini's* saviour on the hills, seemed to appear before her again, and this time like a stern dispenser of justice asked her to cross the river. There was no means to go to the other side of the river—there was neither boat nor bridge. The man, however, said in a stern voice, "Swim across the river, thou wretched creature. Thou knowest to swim very well—thou hadst enough of swimming with *Pratap*, in the *Ganges*."

How could *Shaibalini* make up her mind to plunge into that awful river of blood? The man, finding her hesitating to obey his mandate, raised the rod in his hand to strike her. In great fear, poor *Shaibalini* saw that the rod was made of red-hot iron. Finding her still delaying to obey his command, the man began to strike her severely with that awful instrument of torture. *Shaibalini* got scorched under those fearful strikes. Unable to bear the pains of that horrible infliction, she threw herself into that river of blood. Forthwith, those strange and fearful crocodiles rushed towards her, but they did not seize her. She began to swim; the current of blood was entering into her mouth, and occasionally rotten dead bodies, emitting a most noxious smell, came floating upon her. The extraordinary man was following her closely. He, however, had not to swim—he walked over the river. In this way, *Shaibalini* arrived at the other side of the river. She got up on the bank, and repeatedly cried out for help, at the sight of some fearful object before her. What she saw before her had no limit, no shape, no colour and no name. There the light was very dim, but it was yet so very intense that it produced a most painful burning effect upon *Shaibalini's* eyes—it was like the burning sensation of some deadly venom. So foul and offensive was the smell there that although *Shaibalini* had covered her nose with her cloth, it made her painfully restless. A horrible mixture of confused sounds was entering into her ears—heart-rending wails, fearful laughter, terrible howls of supernatural beings, deafening noise of cracking hills, tumultuous roars of thunder, boisterous clamour of gushing streams and dreadful hissings of blazing fire, all these pierced into her ears. At times, such a violent gust of hot wind was blowing against her that she felt she was passing through flames. Then again, at intervals, a most biting cold was inflicting upon her the pains of a thousand dagger. *Shaibalini* in a voice of agony began to cry out, "Oh, save me—I can bear no more." While she was thus crying for help, in that horrible plight, a large loathesome worm, emitting an unbearable noxious smell, began to wind its way into her mouth. At this most painful and hideous torture, *Shaibalini* cried out, at the top of her voice, "Oh save me—I am thrown into Hell! Is there no means to get out of it?"

"Yes, there is," replied *Shaibalini's* tormentor.

Shaibalini was roused from her torpor by the shrieks she had burst into, in her horrible dream. But even then, she was under the influence of the vision she had seen and so although awake, she cried out,

"Oh, what will be my fate! Is there no means for my redemption?"

"Yes there is," replied a deep sombre voice from within the cave.

What, was *Shaibalini* actually in Hell? Startled and slightly frightened too, at this unexpected but awe-inspiring reply, *Shaibalini* asked,

"What will save me from this misery?"

That strange voice was again heard within the cave. It prescribed, as a penance for her sins, a religious vow, which she was to observe for twelve years. Was this actually a voice from Heaven?

"What is that vow and who will teach me how to observe it?" inquired poor *Shaibalini*, in a piteous voice.

"I shall teach you," was the reply of the unseen preceptor.

"Who are you?" Asked *Shaibalini*, encouraged at the hope of her salvation.

"Listen to what I say," was the only reply.

"What am I to do?" inquired *Shaibalini* in resignation.

"Take off your *Saree*, and wear what I give you instead," said the unknown voice. "Stretch out your hand to receive it."

Shaibalini held out her hand, as enjoined, and a piece of cloth was placed on her palm. She changed her *Saree*, and asked,

"What else am I to do?"

Answer. Where is your father-in-law's house?

Shaibalini. It is at *Bedagram*. Shall I have to go there?

Answer. Yes, go there and raise a hut for your habitation at the outskirt of the village.

Shaibalini. What else?

Answer. Don't use any bed—you must lie on the bare ground.

Shaibalini. Anything more?

Answer. You shall live upon fruits and herbs only. Don't take more than one meal a day.

Shaibalini. Then?

Answer. Neglect your hair so that they may grow matted like those of an ascetic.

Shaibalini. Is this all?

Answer. No, one thing more. You shall enter into the village, only once a day, for alms, and recount your sinful story, as you beg from door to door.

Shaibalini. Oh! my story is not to be told to any one. Is there no other form of penance?

Answer. Yes, there is.

Shaibalini. What is that?

Answer. Death.

Shaibalini. Yes, this will suit me—I will die. Who are you, please?

Shaibalini got no reply. She then said in a piteous voice, "Whoever you may be, I need not know it. I take you to be the presiding deity of these hills and make obeisance to you. Be pleased to give me one more information. Where is my husband now?"

Answer. Why do you want to know of it?

Shaibalini. Will it not be my lot to see him again?

Answer. You will see him when you have undergone the penance, I first prescribed for you.

Shaibalini. After twelve long years?

Answer. Yes, after twelve years.

Shaibalini. How long shall I stand this ordeal—If I die within these twelve years?

Answer. Then you will see him at the time of your death.

Shaibalini. Is there nothing which can enable me to see him before that? You are a divine being, and you certainly know of it.

Answer. If you want to see him soon, you shall have to pass seven days and nights in this lonely cave, alone. Think of your husband all day and night, and see that nothing else may creep into your mind. During these seven days, you shall come out of the cave only once in the evening, to gather fruits and herbs for your meals. But see that you do not take much of them, and thus satisfy your hunger fully. In case you meet anybody on the hills, you should not speak to him. If you can stay in this dark cave, for seven days, and continually think of your husband with absolute devotion, you will see him here.

III

The Wind of Virtue Blew

Shaibalini acted up to the advice of her unknown preceptor—she passed seven long days and nights in that dismal cave. She used to come out of it, only once in the day, to gather fruits and herbs for her meals. During those days, she spoke to no human being, as enjoined on her. In that hideous darkness, almost without any food, *Shaibalini* began to think of her husband, with absolute devotion. In her contemplation, she completely lost her perception of the things of the external world. The functions of her mind and organs of senses were suspended for the time, and she saw nothing but her husband, on all sides. He alone became the sole object of her thought. During those seven days and nights, she saw nothing but the face of her husband. In that dreadful silence, she could only hear the wise and affectionate utterances of her lord—her sense of smell could perceive nothing else but the sweet fragrance of the flowers with which he worshipped the deities, and her power of touch could only feel the pleasure of his fond and loving caresses. All her hopes were now concentrated in one particular thing, which was nothing but an earnest desire to behold her husband once again. Like the bee, which even under the smart pricks of thorns, takes delight to wing its favourite course round flowers of rare fragrance and beauty, sweetly smiling from within their thorny environments, *Shaibalini's* mind, inspired by the memory of her lord, began to wander about his face, which wore a manly beauty, with its well-matched pair of moustaches and broad forehead.

The man, who prescribed this form of penance, had undoubtedly deep insight into all the complex workings of the human mind.

In a dark and lonely place, where no human face can be seen, and at a time when the thoughts of this world and its gross affairs are conspicuous by their absence, the mind becomes deeply absorbed in any matter upon which it is fixed. In the midst of those dismal associations, *Shaibalini*, with a weak mind and a weak body, got beside herself in the deep and uninterrupted meditation of her husband.

Was this mental aberration or the awakening of the inner conscience with its supernatural vision?

Shaibalini now saw the image of her husband before her eyes, in the vividness of reality. The moment she saw it, she was charmed by its fascinating beauty and heavenly grace. She thought within herself, "Ay, this fine and stately figure is a faultless creation of beauty! Its broad forehead, with its wrinkles, is verily the sacred seat of wisdom and manliness! What is *Pratap* in comparison with this majestic embodiment of beauty and virtue? Fie on my judgment, I could not so long see the difference between a river and an ocean! Can *Pratap's* eyes be favourably compared with those that adorn the ethereal mould, before me? How bright and beautiful are these large wandering eyes— how tenderly affectionate, how inquisitively enquiring and how calm yet sportive are their charming glances! Ah me, why did I not see all these before—Why did I run mad after a fond delusion, and bring about my own ruin! Oh, what a striking combination of delicate beauty with stern manliness is there in the majestic appearance of my beloved lord! Ah, who can say what it is most like! Tall and beautiful as the stately oak with its green mantles, grand and lovely like the towering pine in the sweet embraces of winding creepers, lofty and imposing like the mountain with its fascinating garlands of wild flowers, bright as the glaring light of the glorious sun and refreshing, at the same time, like the silvery radiance of the gentle moon—it stands unparalleled in its grace and loveliness. I now see, with a clear vision, that the gods have lent my noble husband all their heavenly grace and virtue, and the goddesses all their beauty and sweetness. How poor does *Pratap* look before him, whom I have foolishly neglected so long! Alas, why did I not see all these before—why did I allow my heart to be swayed by my passions, and thus fall from grace! How sweet and elegant, chaste and enlivening are his gentle and witty words—how soft yet clear and ringing is his magic voice! Alas, why my ears were deaf to its music so long—why did I run away from home, and lose my honour! Ay, his captivating smiles are as beautiful as the sweet jessamine, as bright as the silvery flash of lightning in the blue sky, and as sweet as pleasant dreams in peaceful nights! And his love? Oh, it is as deep as the ocean itself—reposing in the calmness of its majesty, but overflowing at the slightest stir! Ah me, why my eyes were blind to all these so long—why did I not plunge into that ocean of love, and sleep in its placid bosom, quite forgetful of my own existence! Shame, what a trifle I am to him! I am a mere girl, inexperienced and illiterate, wicked and miserably unfit to appreciate his greatness; how can I be worthy of him? What the small shell is to the ocean, what the insignificant worm is to the flower, in the bloom of beauty and fragrance, and what the dark spot is to the glorious moon, my wretched self is to the guardian angel of my life. Yea, I am to him what the dismal gloom of bad dreams is to the life, and blank forgetfulness to the mind. I am the cursed obstacle to his happiness, and a cruel disappointment to his best hopes. Ah me, my alliance with him is like the combination of mud with pure transparent water, or the association of prickly thorns with the soft stalk of lotus, or of the noxious particles of dust with the life-giving breath of Heaven! Alas, why my life did not come to an end when I lost myself in the enchantment of a fond delusion!"

The man who had advised *Shaibalini* to remain absorbed in the meditation of her lord, for seven days and nights, was certainly an unerring pilot in the sea of life—he had by all means a clear vision of all the affairs of this world. He knew that the lesson which he had taught to *Shaibalini*, could turn the current of life from its ever familiar course, and make it flow through a new channel. He knew too that its potency could break the stony indifference to the duties of life, dry up the monstrous sea of sin and immorality, and stop the wild whirlwind of passions.

So *Shaibalini* forgot *Pratap*, and learnt to love *Chandra Shekhar*. Cut the wings of human passions, annihilate the senses altogether, bring the mind completely under your control, rob it of its innate strength, let it run its course through an only -open- channel and you will find that it will follow no other than the prescribed path, and be gradually contented with its changed course and new environment.

On the fifth day of her prescribed penance, *Shaibalini* did not partake of the fruits and herbs she had brought for her meals. On the sixth day, she did not stir out of the cave at all, and on the following morning, she resolved that whether she could see her husband or not, she would surely put an end to her life before the next dawn. In the night, it seemed to *Shaibalini* that a lily of unspeakable beauty bloomed within her heart, and *Chandra Shekhar* was seated on it, in the contemplation of God; she herself was transformed into a bee, and was humming round his lotus feet.

The seventh night of her penance was as horribly dark and silent as the previous ones. In that dismal cave, *Shaibalini* lost her consciousness in the uninterrupted meditation of her lord. She saw visions of various descriptions. Once, it seemed to her, that she was thrown into the fearful abyss of hell, where innumerable snakes of inordinate lengths, with their hoods extended, began to coil round her body—they were, at times, rushing towards her, with their jaws wide open, to swallow her up, and their breaths, all coming together, resembled in their noise a strong gale. It seemed to *Shaibalini* that *Chandra Shekhar* appeared on the scene, and took his stand upon the expanded hood of a large snake; forthwith the serpents vanished away like the receding waters of an ebbing tide. Sometimes, she saw a wide and deep chasm, containing a mountain-high pile of blazing fire—its flames touched the blue vault of the sky overhead; *Shaibalini* was about to be burnt alive in it, when, all on a sudden *Chandra Shekhar* appeared there, and quenched that hellish fire by throwing on it a handful of water. Instantly a balmy breeze blew in that region, and a transparent sheet of water began to flow, in a luxurient and murmuring stream, through that once infernal chasm; flowers of all hues and sweet fragrance seen to adorn the banks of that magic rivulet, and in its water bloomed lotuses of exuberant growth and beauty; *Chandra Shekhar* was seem to float away in that placid current, on one of those beautiful lilies. Then again, it seemed to *Shaibalini* that a huge tiger was carrying her in its mouth, on the top of the hills, when *Chandra Shekhar* came to her rescue and severed the head of the ferocious brute by the single stroke of a flower, which he had brought from his holy place of worship; the face of the tiger resembled that of wicked Foster.

At the close of the seventh night, it appeared to *Shaibalini* that her life was out, but consciousness had not left her. She saw that some hideous infernal beings were rising with her corpse towards the sky above, in that dismal darkness. After some time, she felt that she was being dragged by her hair across innumerable seas of black clouds and through fires of countless flashes of lightning. She saw that fair celestial beings, inhabiting those airy regions, raised their heads above the waves of clouds, and were smiling at *Shaibalini*, in contempt. Elsewhere, she found goddesses of resplendent beauty, bedecked with beautiful garlands of stars and streaks of lightning, sailing through the air, on clouds of golden hue—the halo round their body lost its heavenly lustre as it came in contact with the air, which was polluted by the touch of *Shaibalini's* sinful body. In another part of the sky, she saw, with fear, dreadful monster-like aerial beings, inclining their dark shadow-like huge bodies against black clouds of stupendous magnitude, whirling about with the violent wind that was blowing there. The very moment they got the smell of *Shaibalini's* corpse, their mouths watered, and they rushed towards it to swallow it up, with their fearful jaws wide open. In another direction, she saw images of innumerable chariots of celestial beings cast upon the clouds—their dazzling brilliancy surprised *Shaibalini* beyond measure. The heavenly spirits in them, it seemed, were moving away their chariots in all haste, lest their sacred shadows would come in contact with that of *Shaibalini's* sinful corpse and thereby sanctify her wicked soul. Her eyes next fell upon the sparkling little faces of the beautiful stars, smiling in the blue sky, like so many unveiled beauties of matchless charms; they were, it seemed, pointing out to one another the corpse of *Shaibalini*, with their little glittering fingers. Some of those shining luminaries closed their twinkling eyes at the very sight of an earthly sinner—many hid their bright faces behind the clouds, and others vanished away in dark obscurity, shocked at the horror of the scene.

The dreadful infernal carriers of *Shaibalini's* corpse, it seemed, were still rising higher and higher to hurl down their charge into the horrible abyss of hell. At last they arrived at a place where there was no light, no darkness, no cloud and no air. There was no sound too, but all on a sudden a tumultuous rumbling noise came to that region from far below—it seemed, as if, a thousand oceans roared simultaneously. The goblins of hell, in charge of *Shaibalini's* body, at once cried out, "Hark! there comes the noise of hell—let us hurl down the corpse from here." They then let fall the corpse with a kick on its head. *Shaibalini's* dead body, it seemed to her poor fear-stricken soul, was now rolling down and down, through an endless blank of nothingness—the whirling speed with which it was falling increased by rapid strides, with every moment, till at last the corpse began to revolve like the potter's wheel, working in full motion. Blood came out of its mouth and nostrils profusely. The rattling tumult and commotion of hell was heard nearer, and the noxious smell from its hideous dens became more and more unbearable. Then all on a sudden, the dead but nevertheless conscious *Shaibalini* saw before her eyes the fearful infernal regions, where the wicked are punished after death. Immediately after this she lost her sight, and her ears became deaf. Now she turned all her thoughts to her husband, and invoked his presence to save her from the horrible tortures of hell. She said, "Where art thou, my lord *Chandra Shekhar*, the guardian angel of my life, the god of my idolatry and the dispenser of my weal and happiness—where art thou at this hour of misfortune! I fall prostrate before thy lotus feet—oh save me! I am being thrown into that hell before me, for my sinful conduct towards you, and no god can avert my doom unless you come to my rescue—oh save me! If you will only come and place your feet on my head, I shall be saved from eternal damnation. Oh, take pity on me, and come to my rescue!"

Shaibalini then felt that some one took her up on his lap very gently—the fragrance of his body filled the air all around with a pleasant odour. The horrible tumult of hell was suddenly hushed into silence, and the breeze which was hitherto carrying the foul smell of that hideous region of doom and damnation, now brought forth sweet and delightful scent of fragrant flowers. All on a sudden, *Shaibalini's* lost sight was restored to her, and her ears resumed their natural functions. She felt all at once that she was not dead but alive, and that what she saw was not altogether an illusive vision. *Shaibalini* regained her consciousness. She opened her eyes, and found that a faint light had crept into that dismal cave; outside, was heard the morning melody of birds. But then, what was this—on whose lap was her head resting—whose face was it that hung over her like the silvery disc of the glorious moon, shedding light in that fast-disappearing darkness of the early dawn? *Shaibalini* recognised who it was—he was no other than *Chandra Shekhar* himself, in the garb of a hermit!

IV

The Wreck of Sin

Chandra Shekhar called out, "*Shaibalini!*"

Shaibalini got up, and sat by him. She then fixed her eyes upon his face, and instantly fell on the ground, overpowered with emotion; her lips touched his feet, as if, to beg his forgiveness with a kiss. *Chandra Shekhar* raised her up, and made her sit, supporting her feebled body on his arms. *Shaibalini* began to weep loudly, and again fell on *Chandra Shekhar's* feet—she said, "Oh! What will be my fate now!"

"Why did you want to see me!" inquired *Chandra* Shekhar *calmly.*

Shaibalini controlled her tears and wiped her eyes. She then said in an exceedingly calm and sombre voice, "It seems, I shall not live long."

Shaibalini now shuddered at the recollection of what she saw in her dreams. Resting her head on her little palm, she remained silent for a time and then said,

"My life has only a few days more to run out, and so my desire to see you, before my death, became very strong within me. But. then, who will believe in what I say, and why should people believe me at all? How can the fallen woman, who has forsaken her husband, sincerely wish to behold her lord again?" *Shaibalini* then burst into an unnatural laughter, indicative of her grief and remorse.

"There is no reason to disbelieve you," said *Chandra Shekhar* in an exceedingly kind manner. "I know that you were forcibly taken away from home."

"Is it a sin to commit suicide?" suddenly inquired *Shaibalini*. She then fixed her eyes upon *Chandra Shekhar*—they were full of tears, and looked like two beautiful lilies floating on water.

Chandra Shekhar. Yes, it is a great sin. Why do you want to put an end to your life?

All on a sudden *Shaibalini* again shuddered, and said, "No, my heart fails, I cannot court death; I fear, I shall fall into that horrible hell before me!"

Chandra Shekhar. You will be saved from the tortures of hell, if you undergo a penance for your sins.

Shaibalini. What form of penance can save me from the tortures of the hell that is within me?

Chandra Shekhar. What do you mean?

Shaibalini. These hills are visited by divine beings; I cannot say what mysterious change they have brought in me—I dream hell all day and night.

Chandra Shekhar noticed that *Shaibalini's* eyes were fixed upon some object in the direction of the entrance to the cave—it seemed, she was looking at it very closely. He saw that her already pale face was growing paler and her eyes were getting dilated more and more every moment—she began to take hurried and heavy breaths, and every hair of her body stood on its end, as she began to shiver, perhaps, with fear.

Chandra Shekhar asked, "What is it, you are looking at, so minutely?"

Shaibalini made no answer—she was staring, as before. *Chandra Shekhar* again asked,

"What makes you tremble with fear?"

Shaibalini kept mute like a statue. *Chandra Shekhar* was surprised—he looked *Shaibalini* in the face for a time, but could not understand anything. All on a sudden *Shaibalini* burst into a fearful scream—she cried out in a piteous voice,

"My lord, save me—save me from the impending danger! You are my husband and my protector; who else can save me if you do not come to my help?" Immediately, as she concluded, *Shaibalini* fainted, and fell on the ground.

Chandra Shekhar fetched water from the nearest spring and began to sprinkle it on *Shaibalini's* face—he also began to fan her by means of his sheet. A little after, *Shaibalini* regained her consciousness—she sat up, and began to weep in silence. *Chandra Shekhar* then asked,

"What have you been seeing all this time?"

"The hell!" replied *Shaibalini* briefly, in a fear-stricken voice.

Chandra Shekhar felt that *Shaibalini* had been suffering from the tortures of hell, though alive. After a while *Shaibalini* said,

"I cannot make up my mind to die—I am awfully afraid of hell. The moment my life will be out, I shall be thrown into that horrible region of torture. Anyhow I must live; but how can I live alone for twelve long years? Oh, the hideous vision of hell is before me, both when I am conscious or otherwise."

Chandra Shekhar said, "Don't be afraid—continued fasting and mental afflictions have caused all these horrible dreams. Physicians will ascribe them to weakness of brain. You had better go to *Bedagram* and build a hut at the outskirt of the village. *Sundari* will come there and look after you—she will also be able to arrange for your treatment."

Shaibalini did not say anything—she closed her eyes, and saw, before her, the image of *Sundari*, standing at one extremity of the cave, in a threatening attitude. What was more strange, it seemed to her that *Sundari's* stature gradually grew bigger, till at last it attained the height of a stalwart oak—she wore an awfully hideous and horrible appearance. It appeared to the diseased mind of poor *Shaibalini* that she was actually beholding, at the entrance to the cave, the hell with all its fearful associations—the noxious smell of rotten carcasses which she had been smelling in her dreams before—the same fearful hissings of blazing fire—the same painful sensation of heat and cold—that very mysterious legion of snakes, and lastly the very same hideous worms which seemed to have clouded the sky by their number—began to torment her again! The terrible infernal beings again appeared before her and this time with a rope made of prickly thorns and a fearful rod of scorpions—they bound down *Shaibalini* with that mysterious rope, and began to strike her with the deadly instrument of torture in their hand, as they dragged her away along with them. The stalwart figure of *Sundari*, it seemed to *Shaibalini*, raised her hands and shouted to the hellish beings, "Strike—strike her with your rod of torture. I repeatedly asked her to come away with me from *Foster's budgrow*, but she did not follow my advice. So, inflict on her as much pain as you can. I am an eye-witness to her sins, and so I say, punish her wicked soul with all your infernal tortures." *Shaibalini* with folded hands, her face turned upward, and her eyes streaming with tears, was imploring for mercy; but the strange and stern figure of *Sundari* would not listen to her entreaties, and seemed to shout as before, "Strike—strike hard that fallen woman. I am chaste and virtuous, whereas she is a traitor to her husband."

Shaibalini's eyes became dilated, and her face grew pale at the strange vision before her, and she remained silent in dumb surprise, with vacant looks. *Chandra Shekhar* became anxious—he fully understood that all these were the first symptoms of a lurking malady. He said,

"*Shaibalini*! Come along with me."

At first, *Shaibalini* did not hear him. *Chandra Shekhar* then touched her body to draw her attention, and repeatedly asked her to follow him; *Shaibalini* suddenly stood up, and with a fear-stricken voice said,

"Don't delay—hasten off—let us quit this place at once" Forthwith as she concluded, she ran towards the entrance to the cave—*Chandra Shekhar* followed her with quick steps; in her attempt to get away quickly, in the dim light within the cave, her feet struck against a stone, and she fell down on the ground. After that, she said no word and uttered no sound. *Chandra Shekhar* found that *Shaibalini* had fainted again. He took her up on his arms, and carried her to that lovely cool spot outside the cave, where a little fountain was pouring out its water, with a murmuring melody. *Chandra Shekhar* began to sprinkle the cool and refreshing water of that mountain-spring over her face. This palliative and also the fresh life-giving breeze in that lovely open space, soon restored to *Shaibalini* her lost consciousness.

"Where am I now?," inquired *Shaibalini*, as she opened her eyes.

"I have brought you out of the cave," replied *Chandra Shekhar* in a gentle voice.

All on a sudden *Shaibalini* again shuddered—fear again seized her—in an unnatural voice she asked, "Who are you?"

Chandra Shekhar too got frightened—he said, "What is it that upsets you so much? Why can't you recognise me? Look here, I am your husband."

Shaibalini laughed aloud, and said,

> *"My sweet love like the golden flies,*
> *From flower to flower their sweetness tries;*
> *Have you dear, your fond path forgotten,*
> *And so come to this prickly thorn?—*

Are you *Lawrence Foster?*"

Chandra Shekhar could feel that the Goddess of consciousness, who adorn the human nature and lends it that charm and grace which characterise it, was about to leave *Shaibalini*, and a hideous madness was gradually occupying what was once Her holy temple of gold. *Chandra Shekhar* wept a little. He then in an exceedingly mild and endearing tone began to call *Shaibalini* repeatedly by her name. *Shaibalini* again burst into a shrill unnatural laughter, and said,

"Who is *Shaibalini*? Stay, let me reflect! Yes, there was a girl whose name was *Shaibalini*, and there was a boy whose name was *Pratap*; one night the boy was suddenly transformed into a snake, and the girl into a frog, and they both entered into a Jungle. The snake afterwards swallowed up the frog; I have seen it with my own eyes. Well, are you *Lawrence Foster?*"

Chandra Shekhar, in a voice surcharged with deep emotions, exclaimed, "Oh, my venerable preceptor! what is this? Oh! What have you done?"

Shaibalini now sang,

> *"My life's sweet and beloved mate,*
> *Thou hast, by trapping in thy net*
> *The wily charmer of my heart,*
> *Made love's stream to overflow its skirt."*

She then said, "Who is the charmer of my heart? It is *Chandra Shekhar*. Who has been caught in the trap? *Chandra Shekhar*. What is flooded? *Chandra Shekhar*. What are the two banks? I know not. Well, do you know *Chandra Shekhar?*"

Chandra Shekhar breathed a deep sigh, and said, "Can't you recognise me? I am *Chandra Shekhar*."

Shaibalini threw herself upon him and clasped him in her arms. She did not say a word, and began to weep—she wept bitterly—her tears drenched him completely. *Chandra Shekhar* too wept much.

"I will go with you," said *Shaibalini* weeping.

"Come, let us go," said *Chandra Shekhar* in a consoling voice.

"You won't beat me?" inquired *Shaibalini* in a piteous tone.

"Certainly not", replied *Chandra Shekhar*, feelingly.

Chandra Shekhar rose up with a sigh—*Shaibalini* too got up. He then proceeded with a heavy heart, and poor distracted *Shaibalini* followed him. She cried, laughed and sang as she went on.

PART V
THE VEIL

I

The Fate of Amyatt

A Myatt's boat reached *Murshidabad* in due course of time. The *Nawab's* representative, *Mahammad Taki Khan*, was at once informed of it. He came to meet *Amyatt* in his boat, with great pomp. *Amyatt* was greatly pleased at this mark of courtesy. At the close of the interview, *Taki Khan* invited *Amyatt* to dinner. *Amyatt* was persuaded to accept the invitation, but he did so not with a cheerful mind. On the other hand, *Mahammad Taki Khan* secretly stationed sentries to watch, from their hiding places, the boats of the English, so that they might not escape.

When *Mahammad Taki* left *Amyatt's* boat, the Englishmen began to discuss among themselves, whether they should attend the invitation. *Golston* and *Johnson* said that Englishmen did not and should not know what fear is, and so they must join the dinner. *Amyatt*, however, said that when they were about to enter into a war with the *Nawab*, and when ill feelings between the two parties had reached their climax, there was absolutely no necessity to observe ceremonious courtesy. *Amyatt* decided that they should not go to dine at *Taki Khan's* place.

The news of the invitation reached the boat in which *Dalani* and *Kulsam* were being kept as prisoners. *Dalani* and *Kulsam*, thereupon, began to speak with each other, in whispers.

"*Kulsam*, do you hear? I think our deliverance is near at hand", said *Dalani* with a cheerful countenance.

"Why?" inquired *Kulsam*.

Dalani. You don't seem to understand anything, as if you are a simpleton! Don't you see there is something very significant about this invitation, or why should the *Nawab's* men invite those who have carried away the *Begum*? Methinks, these devils will meet with death today.

Kulsam. Has that cheered you up?

Dalani. Why not? I, of course, wish that there may not be any bloodshed, but I cannot but be rather delighted than sorry, if my deliverance follows the death of those, who have unjustly imprisoned me.

Kulsam. But then, why should you be at all so anxious for your deliverance? The Englishmen do not seem to have any other motive than to merely keep us under arrest—they are not molesting us in any way. They have simply imprisoned us, and we women will be imprisoned wherever we may go.

Dalani was greatly annoyed, and she said,

"If I have to live like a captive in my own house, I shall still be regarded there as *Dalani Begum*; but here I am no better than a poor slave girl. It sickens me to talk with you. Now, can you say, why the Englishmen have imprisoned us?"

Kulsam. Why, they have already given out their mind! We are here as much a security for the *Nawab's* good conduct, as *Mr. Hay* is at *Monghyr* for that of the English. We shall be released as soon as *Mr. Hay* is let off; if *Mr. Hay* is left unmolested, we have nothing to be afraid of.

Dalani got more annoyed and said,

"I have nothing to do whatsoever with your *Hay*—I am quite tired of your partiality for the English. Methinks, you will not, perhaps, leave these rogues even if you are let off!"

Kulsam did not show temper; she said with a smile,

"If I do not, would you, in that case, go away without me?"

Dalani was getting more and more short of her temper, and she indignantly said,

"Do you even wish that?"

"Who can say what Fate has ordained for us?" said *Kulsam* with affected seriousness.

At this *Dalani* contracted her eyebrows, and shook her little fist at *Kulsam*; she, however, reserved the blow for the present. She simply raised her clenched fist as far as that cluster of her curls, which hung over her ear like the hovering bee over a beautiful flower. She then said in a rather disgusting tone,

"Would you tell me the truth—why did *Amyatt*, on two different days, called you before him?"

Kulsam. I have already told you all about it—he sent for me only to inquire whether you were quite comfortable here. It is his desire, that so long as we shall have to live with him, we may pass our days comfortably. May God so grant it that the English may not leave us!

Dalani now raised her little closed fist still higher, and said,

"May God so ordain that death may come upon you soon."

Kulsam. If the English let us off, we shall fall into the hands of the *Nawab*—he may forgive you, but I can very well see, that he will by no means let me go unpunished. I always think, that if I get shelter somewhere, I shall no more appear before the *Nawab*, in his Royal Court.

Dalani got herself softened, and said in a voice of emotion,

"But, I know of no other stay than my beloved lord. If I am to die, I will like to breathe my last at his feet."

On the other hand, *Amyatt* ordered his *Sepoys* to get themselves ready for a fight. *Johnson* said to *Amyatt*,

"We are not very strong here—isn't it desirable to take our boat close to the Residency?"

"The hope of founding British rule in India will completely vanish away when an Englishman will, like a coward, take to heels in terror of the natives of this country", said *Amyatt* boastingly. "If we simply remove our boats from this place, the *Mahamedans* will think that we have been frightened by them. It is a thousand times better to stand here and meet death, than to run away in fear; but *Foster* is ill and bedrid—he is unfit to die with sword in hand; so, order him to go to the Residency. Ask the *Begum* and the other woman to go with him and let two *Sepoys* accompany them—it is quite useless for them to stay in the field of action."

After the *Sepoys* had got themselves ready, they hid themselves within the boat, at *Amyatt's* command. There was no dearth of small holes in the matted walls of the country-boats, and so, near each hole a *Sepoy* knelt down with his gun, to fire at the enemies, unobserved. *Dalani* and *Kulsam* got up on *Foster's* boat, as enjoined on them by *Amyatt*. *Foster* left with them for the Residency, with two *Sepoys* guarding his boat. The scouts of *Mahammad Taki* saw this, and went to their chief to inform him of it.

When *Mahammad Taki* heard of this, and found that the Englishmen did not turn up at his place at the appointed hour, he sent a messenger to *Amyatt's* boat to bring along with him the invited Englishmen. *Amyatt*, however, told the man that for reasons of his own, he was unwilling to alight from his boat.

The messenger, thereupon, came away from *Amyatt's* boat, and after having had gone a little off from it, gave an alarm by a blank fire. With that sound were instantly heard the reports of about a dozen guns. Forthwith, *Amyatt* found that shots from the enemy's ranks were coming upon his boat like hails, and that through some places, the enemy's bullets were actually making their way within it.

Now, the *Sepoys* of the English replied to their enemy's guns, and the incessant fires from both sides created a tremendous noise. The

Mahamedans lay concealed behind trees and houses on the bank of the river, and the Englishmen with their *Sepoys*, placed themselves under the cover of their boats. Under such circumstances, no tangible result, except a mere waste of powder, could be expected. The *Mahamedans* lost their patience and violently rushed towards *Amyatt's* boat with sabres and spears in their hands, bursting into fearful shouts, as they came. This, however, did not frighten the resolute Englishmen. With a firm and unyielding attitude, *Amyatt, Golston* and *Johnson* opened an incessant fire on the *Mahamedans*, as they were quickly descending the sandy mound of the river, and at each fire, the brave Englishmen caused one of their enemies to lie for ever on that bed of sand. But, as wave after wave is seen to roll forward in a sea or a mighty river, so, row after row of *Mahamedans* were found to descend the bank of the river. *Amyatt* then shouted to his comrades,

"There is now absolutely no chance of our deliverence. Come, let us then lay down our lives in killing the heretics before us."

No sooner had *Amyatt* concluded, than a few of the *Mahamedans* leaped upon *Amyatt's* boat. The Englishmen, it seemed, were ready for it, and they let off their guns at the assailants all at once—they were blown off from the boat and scattered into the river in all directions. But more *Mahamedans* now got up on the boat, and others began to strike its bottom with heavy clubs and hammers. The boat soon gave way and water rushed into it with a great noise. *Amyatt* then said to his men,

"Why should we suffer ourselves to be drowned here like dumb helpless cattle? Let us go out and die like soldiers with sword in hand."

Amyatt's comrades responded to his heroic call, and the three undaunted Englishmen came out of the boat with sword in hand, and took their stand before a legion of enemies. One of the *Mahamedans* approached *Amyatt* and said to him, with a salute,

"Why should you unnecessarily risk your life? Better come along with us."

"We are determined to die here and not to surrender," replied *Amyatt* with undaunted courage. "If we die here today, a fire will be kindled in *Hindusthan*, which will reduce to ashes the *Moslem* Empire. If this field be moistened with our blood, the royal ensign of *George III* will be easily planted on it."

"Then die", said the *Mahamedan*, and with a single stroke of his sword severed *Amyatt's* head from his body.

Golston saw this, and with a swift hand cut off the head of that dashing enemy, to avenge *Amyatt's* death. Instantly, about a dozen of the *Nawab's* men encircled *Golston* and *Johnson*, and began to strike them severely. The two unfortunate Englishmen soon fell never to rise again!

II

The Stalwart Man Again

After *Pratap* had left with *Foster's Budgrow*, on the night *Shaibalini* was rescued, the men on the cargo boat, carrying arms and ammunition of the English, jumped into the river and picked up *Foster*, who being struck by *Ramcharan's* deadly shot, was floating away very close to that boat, in an unconscious state. *Amyatt* was instantly informed of it and he came there to see *Foster*. He found that *Foster* was completely unconscious, but was still alive. He had sustained a severe injury on his head, and had, therefore, lost his consciousness. There was greater probability of the case taking a fatal turn, but there was still some hope for *Foster's* life. *Amyatt* was a bit of a doctor, and he began to treat *Foster* as best as he could. According to *Bakaullah's* information, a search was made for *Foster's Budgrow*, and the boat, on being found, was brought to the *Ghat*, at *Monghyr*. When *Amyatt* left *Monghyr*, he took with him *Foster*, in that *Budgrow*.

Foster was destined to live longer, and so he recovered under Amyatt's treatment. Again, it was, perhaps, the decree of his fate which saved him from the hands of the *Mahamedans*, at *Murshidabad*; but then, he was now entirely deprived of that ruthless courage and wild vanity which all along characterized him, till *Shaibalini* was snatched away from him, and he himself was so terribly punished for his villany—he was now weak, dejected and was, in fact, reduced to a mere skeleton. He was now awfully afraid of his life, and was running away in all haste from *Murshidabad*, to save himself from the hands of the enemies. The severe wound which he had sustained on his head also affected his common sense to some extent. He was hurrying away his boat as fast as he could—he was afraid lest the *Mahamedans* would pursue and overtake him. He at first thought, that he would take shelter within the Residency at *Cossimbazar*, but he gave up the idea, as he feared, that the *Mahamedans* might attack it. This was a right guess; for, immediately after the fall of *Amyatt* and his comrades, the *Mahamedans* rushed to *Cossimbazar* and plundered the English Residency there.

Foster passed *Cossimbazar, Farasdanga, Saidabad* and *Rangamati*, yet, he could not shake off the fear of being overtaken by a pursuing enemy.

Any boat which he found coming from behind, he fancied, belonged to the *Mahamedans*.

Foster noticed that a little boat was following his *Budgrow*, it seemed to him, persistently. At this, he began to think out a means, by which he could effect an escape. His diseased brain suggested one and a hundred ways by which, he believed, he could save himself from the hands of the pursuing enemy. He once thought, that the best thing for him would be, to leave the boat and escape by land. But, at the very next moment, he felt that it was quite impossible for him to run away— he was physically unfit to do so. Again, it occured to his diseased mind, that he would be safe if he would jump into the water. But, he instantly perceived that it would mean his death as well. He next thought, that his boat would go faster if he would cast into the river the two women with him.

All on a sudden, *Foster* jumped into another conclusion, which forced itself on him through his perverted understanding. It was, now, his firm belief, that the *Mahamedans* were pursuing him so tenaciously, only to rescue the two women in his boat. He had come to know that *Dalani* was the *Nawab's Begum*, and he thought that the enemies were continuing the chase for her alone. It, therefore, seemed to him that everything would be all right, if he would let off the *Begum*. He finally decided that he would drop down *Dalani*, somewhere on the bank of the river. He then said to the *Begum*,

"Do you see that yonder little boat, following us?"

"Yes, I do," replied *Dalani*, briefly.

"That boat belongs to your party," said *Foster*. "It is coming to snatch you off from our hands."

Was there really any reason to justify such a suspicion? No, nothing of the kind. It was absolutely the outcome of *Foster's* mental aberration— he mistook a rope for a snake. If *Dalani* had carefully considered what *Foster* had said, she would have certainly questioned the reality of *Foster's* apprehension. But, it is invariably the case that people completely lose themselves in the fascination of the very name of the object they crave for—hope makes them blind and they unhesitatingly shun deliberation! *Dalani's* mind was completely captivated by the hope, which *Foster's* words about her prospective deliverance, had inspired within her, and so she believed every word of *Foster*. She said to him,

"If what you say is true, why not let that boat come near us, so that we may get into it? If you will do so, I will amply reward you."

"By God, I cannot do that," said *Foster*. "If your men can once get hold of me, they will surely put an end to my life."

"I will prevent them from doing you any harm," replied *Dalani* with charming innocence.

"They will not listen to you," said *Foster*. "The people of your country have no regard for women's word!"

"In that case, you better drop us down on the shore, and go away," suggested *Dalani*, with her usual simplicity.

Dalani lost her sense through extreme impatience. She could not, therefore, carefully consider the good and evil of what she was going to do. She did not think, even for a moment, that she would be quite in a wide sea, if the boat, suspected to be the *Nawab's*, were actually not his; it did not, in fact, at all come to her mind that the boat might not be of the *Nawab*. She lost her patience, and plunged herself into a great peril. *Foster* was only too glad to agree to her alternative proposal, and he ordered his men to take his boat to the shore.

Kulsam, however, said, "I will by no means get down. If the *Nawab* can once get hold of me, I do not know what punishment he may not inflict on me. I will go to Calcutta with the *Sahib*—I have acquaintances there."

"You need not be afraid in the least," said *Dalani* in an impressively assuring tone. "If I live, I will also save you."

"Ay, if you live at all!" said *Kulsam* in reply.

Nothing could persuade *Kulsam* to get down from the boat with *Dalani*. The *Begum* repeatedly implored *Kulsam* to accompany her, but to no purpose.

"You too better get down," said *Foster* to *Kulsam*. "Who can say that the *Nawab's* men will not continue the chase if you be with me?"

"If you will drop me down here," said *Kulsam* with a fine cunningness, "I will do all that I can to persuade the *Nawab's* men not to let you escape—I will see that they do not give up pursuing you."

Kulsam's threat had its effect on *Foster's* mind and he did not dare to meddle with her any more.

Dalani shed tears for *Kulsam*, and alighted from the boat, alone. *Foster* left the place forthwith, and hastened off, as fast as he could. The portals of the day were then about to be closed, and the moment was fast approaching when the mighty Sun was to retire from his day's work, to rest behind the horizon.

Foster's boat soon got out of sight. The little boat, which *Foster* had taken to be the *Nawab's*, now drew nearer—every moment, *Dalani* thought that it would be brought to the shore, to take her away on it. But it did not so happen. Suspecting that the men in the boat had not seen her, *Dalani* raised one end of her *Shari*, and began to wave it to and fro. But inspite of this, the boat was not brought to the shore and it passed her away. It was then that a doubt flashed through her mind, like a quick streak of lightning, that the boat which she had taken to be the *Nawab's* might not be his, and it was quite possible that it belonged to some other person altogether! *Dalani* then became almost mad, and began to call aloud the men in that boat. "There is no room in this boat," was the only reply they made and rowed away.

Dalani now felt that a thunder-bolt had come upon her. *Foster's* boat was then out of sight—yet she ran, as fast as she could, along the bank, in the hope that she would be able to overtake it. She ran a great distance, but she could not even catch a glimpse of *Foster's Budgerow*. The sun had already gone down the horizon, and now every object was enveloped by the falling shade of night. Nothing could be seen on the wide expanse of the river, as far as the vision of man could go; only the boisterous tumult of the flowing *Bhagirathi*, now swollen to the very edge of its banks, on account of the fresh and luxuriant supply of the rains, could be heard, in that dismal darkness. In utter despair, *Dalani* sat down on that dreary and isolated bank of the river, like a torn creeper!

After a while, *Dalani* felt that it was quite useless for her to remain there. She, therefore, got up and began to ascend the steep bank of the river. In that hideous darkness it was quite possible to find out a way of easy access, and so she stumbled and fell down several times before she could get on the main land. She then looked around and found that there was no trace of a village, as far as she could see, in the dim light of the twinkling stars overhead—she could only see a desolate field of endless dimension and the wide expanse of the *Ganges*, untiringly running its course with incessant murmurs. Not to speak of a man, she could not even see a faint light, a tree or a track in any direction. Only the beautiful images of the sparkling stars could be seen dancing in the waving ripples of the flowing *Bhagirathi. Dalani* felt that her end had surely come.

In that fearful lonely place, not far off from the river, *Dalani* took her seat, in utter despair. The drowsy hum of the beetles and the yell of jackals could be heard very close to her. Gradually the night advanced and with it the darkness became denser and more hideous. In the dead of night *Dalani* saw, with fear, a stalwart man, moving about, alone, in that desolate region. The man drew near *Dalani* and sat by her, without speaking a word.

The stalwart man again! He was no other than that mysterious person who had ascended the hills with *Shaibalini* on his arms, during the furious storm which had burst forth on the mountainous region, where unfortunate *Shaibalini* had been cast by the cruel tyranny of fate!

III

The Dance

Sarupchand and his brother *Mahatab-Chand Jagatsetts* were residing in their palatial residence, at *Monghyr*. Within that magnificent mansion, there were burning, on that night, a thousand lamps of dazzling brilliancy. The countless rays of those brilliant lights were being most charmingly reflected by the dazzling ornaments of the dancing girl, within the marble hall. The flow of water is most effectually arrested by a barrier of water itself, and so brilliancy is best retained by a bright object. The shooting beams from those glowing lamps were, therefore, glittering in a most beautiful and striking manner on the bright marble pillars—the gorgeous *Musnad*, with its sparkling jewels and golden embroidery—the most artistically carved scent receptacles of every shape and variety, set with brilliants of the first water, and lastly on the charming necklaces of large and well-shaped pearls of the purest colour, which adorned the princely hosts. In the midst of that dazzling magnificence, was issuing forth the sweet and melodious voice of the dancing girl. The splendour of the glowing lights and the sweet flow of that delicious music, produced a most harmonious combination of brilliancy and sweetness. When the moon appears on the blue sky of the night—when the sparkling waters of the *Ganges* under her silvery radiance, being stirred by the gentle breeze, breaks into ripples, which too sparkle in that beautiful light, or when the most pleasant and life-giving southern breeze enhances the refreshing beauty of a silvery night, we notice the same striking combination of brilliancy and sweetness. Again, when the long golden rays of the morning sun, slowly and gently unfold the petals of the budding lilies, smiling on the blue transparent waters of a pond—when those gentle and slanting beams light up each particle of water on the green leaves of the lotus stalk, and strike, so to speak, the morning notes of the aquatic birds, or inspire the gay and frolicsome cuckoo of the spring to pour forth upon this world a flood of melody, we notice that very charming combination of brilliancy and sweetness. Then again, when beautiful glances flash like the inconstant streaks of lightning from the dark blue eyes of a bashful beauty, floating like two charming lilies, in the tears of farewell or affected displeasure, or when your sweet-heart, waving her earrings, pours into your ears extremely pleasant and sweet epithets, we notice the same combination of brilliancy and sweetness. Lastly, when the sparkling Champagne glitters in a transparent flask, or when in the brilliant light of a chain of glowing lamps, a sweet damsel, gorgeously bedecked with jewels and draperies, sings merrily, we observe the very same striking combination of brilliancy and sweetness. Such a combination was effected, that night, in the palatial residence of the *Setts'*, but it had no effect on the minds of the two princely brothers—*Gurgan Khan* was the sole object of their thought.

At the time we are speaking of, the devastating fire of war had blazed forth in Bengal. Even before he received any intimation from the Council at *Calcutta, Ellis* had attacked the *Nawab's* Fort, at Patna, and taken it by storm. But subsequently, an army was sent there by the *Nawab*, which effecting a junction with the *Mahamedan* fighters there, retook the fort. *Ellis* and his men fell into the hands of the *Mahamedans*, and were brought to *Monghyr*, as prisoners of war. After that, both sides were preparing for a struggle, in right earnest. *Gurgan Khan* was conferring with the *Jagatsetts* on that momentous subject—the dance was merely an excuse for their meeting; neither the *Jagatsetts* nor *Gurgan Khan* were enjoying it. Their indifference to music, on such an occasion, was by no means unnatural; for, who organizes such a meeting for the sake of dance and music?

Gurgan Khan arrived at a final decision—he thought that when war would exhaust both the parties, he would defeat both the *Nawab* and the English, and install himself on the *Guddee* of Bengal. But the first thing that was required for the accomplishment of such an object, thought *Gurgan Khan*, was to keep the soldiers of the *Nawab* absolutely under his own control. The soldiers, however, would not fight for him unless he could win them over by money. But it was impossible for him to have sufficient funds unless the *Sett* Plutuses would come to his help. It was, therefore, absolutely necessary for *Gurgan Khan* to take the *Jagatsetts* into his confidence, and have with them a conference on that subject. On the other hand, the *Nawab* too knew it very well that any side to which these two immensely rich brothers would lend their support, would ultimately become victorious. He also knew that the *Jagalsetts* were not his well-wishers at heart; for his treatment towards them had been other than good. He was, out of suspicion, detaining them at *Monghyr* almost like prisoners. The *Nawab* was in fact, devising means to imprison them within the Castle, knowing it for certain that they would, whenever opportunity will present itself, go over to the side of his enemies. The *Jagatsetts* had come to know of the *Nawab's* intention. They had not done anything against *Mir Kashim* so long out of fear only. But they now realised that their deliverance would be impossible unless they combined with *Gurgan Khan*—their, as well as *Gurgan Khan's* object being the complete overthrow of *Mir Kashim*. But lest the *Nawab* would suspect *Gurgan Khan* if he would meet them without any occasion for it, they had got up the dance, and invited *Gurgan Khan* to be present on the occasion, along with the other high officials of the *Nawab*.

Gurgan Khan had come there with the *Nawab's* permission, but he did not take his seat with the other officials—he managed to keep himself a little aloof from them. The princely hosts were often coming and conversing with him in the very same way as they were doing with their other guests; but their conversation with *Gurgan Khan* was carried on in an inaudible voice. It was something like this:—

Gurgan Khan. I intend to start a factory jointly with you. Are you ready to be my partners?

Mahatabchand. With what end in view?

Gurgan Khan. To bring the big factory at *Monghyr* to a dead-lock.

Mahatab. Yes, I am quite willing to be your partner—unless we start a business like that we can, by no means, hope to avert our ruin.

Gurgan Khan. If you agree to my proposal you shall have to supply the necessary capital, and I shall combine with it my labour to carry on the business.

At this moment the dancing girl, *Mania Bai*, sang, "Oh thou knowest tricks well. . ." This brought a smile into *Mahatabchand's* lips, and he carelessly enquired, "Whom does she mean? Let it go—now, to what we were saying—we are quite willing to accept your conditions, provided our capital is quite secure with the interest thereon and we are not involved in any difficulty hereafter."

Thus, while the dancing girl was entertaining the assembled guests with a rich variety of Indian tunes, *Gurgan Khan* and the *Jagatsetts* were discussing their plans in words which were intelligible to themselves alone. When everything was settled, *Gurgan Khan* said,

"Have you heard that a new merchant is starting lots of factories in this country?"

Mahatab. No. Is he a native of this country or a foreigner?

Gurgan Khan. Yes, a native.

Mahatab. Where are his factories?

Gurgan Khan. In all the places between *Monghyr* and *Murshidabad*. He is establishing factories wherever there is a hill, a jungle or a waste land.

Mahatab. Is he a big capitalist?

Gurgan Khan. He is not as yet, but it is not possible to say what he will be in the future.

Mahatab. With what factory does he carry on transactions?

Gurgan Khan. With the big factory at *Monghyr*.

Mahatab. Is he a Hindoo or a Musalman?

Gurgan Khan. A Hindoo.

Mahatab. What's his name?

Gurgan Khan. *Pratap Roy*.

Mahatab. Where does he come from?

Gurgan Khan. From the neighbourhood of *Murshidabad*.

Mahatab. I have heard his name—he is an ordinary man.

Gurgan Khan. By God, he is a dangerous man.

Mahatab. What has led him to plunge into this affair?

Gurgan Khan. He bears a severe grudge against the *Calcutta* Factory.

Mahatab. We must bring him over to our side—what can buy him up?

Gurgan Khan. It is not possible to answer this question till we come to know what has set him to this work. If he has undertaken it on mercenary considerations, it will not take much time to win him over; but if there be anything else at the bottom?

Mahatab. What else can it be? What is it that has stirred up so much enthusiasm in him?

At that moment the dancing girl was singing "Oh that fair and sweet face. . ."

Hearing her *Mahatabchand* said,

"Is it so—whose fair face is it?"

IV

What Dalani Did

The stalwart man came and silently took his seat by *Dalani*. She was then weeping, but she controlled her tears out of fear, and remained absolutely silent and motionless. The man too kept perfectly quiet.

Simultaneously with this strange incident, was growing up, elsewhere, a fresh misfortune for *Dalani*!

Mahammad Taki had private instructions from the *Nawab* to anyhow rescue *Dalani Begum* from the hands of the English and send her to *Monghyr*.

Mahammad Taki thought that the deliverance of the *Begum* would follow, as a matter of course, if he could either capture or kill the Englishmen, who had been carrying her away with them. He therefore did not deem it necessary to give any special instruction to his men about the *Begum*. Subsequently, when he found that the *Begum* was not in the boat of the Englishmen, his men had killed, he felt that his position was quite insecure. There was absolutely no knowing what step the *Nawab* might not take against him, to punish his carelessness and negligence of duty. Apprehending the *Nawab's* displeasure and the serious consequences which might follow from it, *Mahammad Taki*, out of fear, made up his mind to deceive the *Nawab*. At that time, it was a wide-spread rumour that as soon as the war would break out, the English would release *Mirzaffer* from his captivity, and again install him on the *Guddee* of Bengal. So *Mahammad Taki* thought that if the English would gain, it would matter very little even if *Mir Kashim* would come to know of the trick he was intending to play with his royal master. Besides, it was absolutely necessary for him to anyhow prevent, at least for the present, any unpleasant order against him. If *Mir Kashim* would beat the *English*, thought *Mahammad Taki*, he would be able to devise means by which the *Nawab* could be kept in the dark about his conduct. Having thus made up his mind to play false with his master, *Mahammad Taki* sent to the *Nawab*, on the very night *Dalani* met the stalwart man on the isolated bank of the *Ganges*, a letter, full of gross and mischievous lies.

He wrote to say that the *Begum* had been found in *Amyatt's* boat and that he had brought her to the fort at *Murshidabad*, where she was now being kept with every mark of honour and respect. But he could not send her to the *Nawab's* royal court without a special order; for, he had come to know from *Amyatt's* servants that the *Begum* had been living with *Amyatt* as his mistress, and the *Begum* herself had admitted her guilt. She has embraced Christianity as her religion and is quite unwilling to go to *Monghyr*. She says, "Let me go away—I will go to Calcutta and live there with *Amyatt's* friends. If you will not let me off, I will seek every opportunity to steal away—if you will send me to *Monghyr* I will commit suicide." Under such circumstances, he could not but await instructions as to whether he would let off the *Begum*—detain her at *Murshidabad*—or send her to *Monghyr*. He would act according to the order he would now receive.

A messenger on horse-back started for *Monghyr* that very night, with that fatal letter.

It is said that misfortunes which are still far off, sometimes cast their shadows on our minds to indicate their approach. It may not be an absolute truth, but at the very moment the messenger left *Murshidabad* with *Mahammad Taki's* letter to the *Nawab*, every hair of *Dalani's* body suddenly stood up on its end, and the stalwart man, by her side, spoke out for the first time. Be it for his voice or the gloom of a fore-shadowed evil or something altogether different, *Dalani* all on a sudden shuddered at that evil moment.

The stalwart man said, "I know you—you are *Dalani Begum*."

Dalani got startled.

The man said, "I know too that you have been thrown into this lonely region by a wicked profligate."

Tears again came out from *Dalani's* eyes, in torrents. The stranger enquired, "Where do you mean to go now?"

Dalani was frightened at the sight of the stalwart figure of her present companion in solitude, but his words dispelled all fear from her mind—she found sufficient reason not to be afraid of him. But nevertheless, she did not reply to the query and began to weep, as before. The man repeated his question, and then *Dalani* said,

"Where shall I go? I have no place in this world to resort to. I have only one place of shelter, but that is far off from this desolate shore—who will take me there?"

"You better banish from your mind your desire to go to the *Nawab* again," replied the man.

"Why?" enquired *Dalani*, in surprise and with great anxiety.

"Evil will betide you if you will do so," was his cruel reply.

Dalani shuddered at this gloomy forecast, and she said, almost choked with emotion, "Let it be so—I must go there; for, I have no other shelter in this world. It is thousand times better to face misfortune and be by the side of one's lord than to be away from him to be safe."

"In that case, come," said the man. "I will take you along with me to *Mahammad Taki* at *Murshidabad*. He will send you to *Monghyr*. But, better listen to my advice—the war has commenced and you should not go there now. The *Nawab* is making necessary arrangements to send the members of his household to the fort at *Ruhidas*."

"Whatever misfortune may befall me, I must go there," said *Dalani* with an impressive determination.

"It is the decree of the inexorable fate that you shall not see *Monghyr* again," was the stern reply of the mysterious man.

Dalani Begum anxiously said, "Who can say what is in store for me? I will go to *Murshidabad* with you. So long as the last spark of life will be in me, I will not give up the hope of beholding my beloved lord again."

"I know that very well," said the stalwart man. "Come with me."

In that dark night, *Dalani* set out for *Murshidabad* with her strange and unknown companion. Poor soul, she was going there to give her life, just as a charmed fly approaches a blazing fire, quite unsuspicious of the impending death!

PART VI
THE CONSUMMATION

I

THE UNTOLD STORY

We will now briefly relate what we ought to have said before. It is already known to our readers that the hermit, we have spoken of, was no other than *Chandra Shekhar* himself.

On the very day *Amyatt* had left *Monghyr* with *Foster, Ramananda Swami* came to know, in course of an inquiry, that *Foster, Dalani Begum* and others had all gone with *Amyatt*. He met *Chandra Shekhar* on the bank of the *Ganges* and informed him of it; he said,

"It is now absolutely useless for you to remain at *Monghyr*. I shall send *Shaibalini* to the sacred city of *Benares*, to undergo a penance there. You have taken a solemn vow to dedicate your life to the service of your fellow beings, and I will like you to practically enter into your great philanthropic career, today. *Dalani Begum* is a virtuous lady—she has now fallen on evil times; you should follow her and make every effort to rescue her, whenever you will find an opportunity to do so. Then again, *Pratap* is one of your best well-wishers—he has fallen into difficulty for your sake—you cannot forsake him, at this critical juncture of his life. So, you should, without any delay, follow him."

Chandra Shekhar expressed a desire to inform the *Nawab* of this, but *Ramananda Swami* advised him not to do so and said that he would see that the *Nawab* might come to know of *Dalani's* fate. In obedience to the command of his spiritual preceptor, *Chandra Shekhar* set out in a small boat, and began to follow *Amyatt. Ramananda Swami* now set himself to find out a trustworthy and reliable disciple, with a view to send with him *Shaibalini* to *Benares*. But all on a sudden, he came to know that *Shaibalini* had left in a small boat and was following *Amyatt. Ramananda Swami* found himself in a great fix—whom was the wicked *Shaibalini* running after—was it *Foster* or *Chandra Shekhar? Ramananda Swami* said within himself, "I fear, I shall again have to concern myself in the gross affairs of this world, for *Chandra Shekhar*". So thinking, he followed the wake of the English, by land.

All through his life, *Ramananda Swami* travelled on foot—he was a hardy pilgrim. He walked along the bank of the river and soon passed *Shaibalini*. He was free from the influences of hunger and sleep and had, in fact, brought them under his control; so, he was able to overtake even *Chandra Shekhar. Chandra Shekhar* saw *Ramananda Swami* on the bank; he came there and made obeisance to his venerable preceptor.

Ramananda Swami said, "I have a mind to go to *Navadwip*, to confer with the learned *Pandits* there; I would better go with you." He got into *Chandra Shekhar's* boat, which left the place forthwith.

When they found the boats of the English lying at anchor, at a distance, they took their little boat to an isolated place by the riverside and alighted from it on the bank. Soon after this, they noticed *Shaibalini's* boat to arrive there, and found that it was taken to another secluded nook, for a halt. *Ramananda Swami* and *Chandra Shekhar* closely observed, from their hiding place, what occurred before their eyes. They saw *Pratap* and *Shaibalini* swimming away from the boat of the English and subsequently making their escape in a boat. As soon as they saw this, they followed *Pratap* and *Shaibalini* in their own boat. After a while they found that *Shaibalini's* boat was taken to the shore— thereupon, they too stopped and remained watching from a distance. *Ramananda Swami* was a man of unlimited wisdom—he asked *Chandra Shekhar*, "Could you make out what conversation took place between *Pratap* and *Shaibalini* while they were swimming away?"

"No," replied *Chandra Shekhar*.

"Then don't go to sleep tonight—keep an eye on them," said *Ramananda Swami*.

Both of them remained awake. In the latter part of the night, they found that *Shaibalini* alighted from her boat and disappeared in the forest on the river-shore. They waited till the small hours of the morning, but *Shaibalini* did not return. It was then that *Ramananda Swami* said to *Chandra Shekhar*,

"Don't you see, there is something very significant in *Shaibalini's* sudden disappearance? She must have gone away with some motive— let us follow her."

Both of them then followed *Shaibalini*, very cautiously. After dusk, *Ramananda Swami* found that the sky was overcast with clouds, and he enquired of *Chandra Shekhar*,

"How much strength do you possess in your arms?"

Chandra Shekhar smiled, and taking up a large block of stone, in one of his hands, threw it off to a good distance.

At this *Ramananda Swami* said, "That's all right—you now go and take your seat somewhere near *Shaibalini*, under a cover—if *Shaibalini* do not get help during the approaching storm, we shall have to see a woman dying before our eyes. There is a cave not far off from this place—I know the way which leads to it—you shall have to follow me there, with *Shaibalini* on your arms, when I shall ask you to do so."

Chandra Shekhar. An impenetrable darkness will soon envelop this place. How shall I see the way?

Ramananda Swami. I shall be very close to you. I shall hold one end of my staff, and the other end will be in your hand.

When *Chandra Shekhar* came out of the cave leaving *Shaibalini* within it, *Ramananda Swami* thought within himself, "I have been studying all through my life the sacred works of divine authority—I have come in contact with all sorts of people and studied life in all its moods—but I see, all in vain! Strange, I have failed to read the mind of this girl! Is there no bottom to this ocean?" He then said to *Chandra Shekhar*, "There is a hill-monastery very close to this place—you better go and rest there tonight. You shall again have to follow *Dalani Begum*, after we have done all that we should, in respect of *Shaibalini*. Know it, you have no other mission in life, except to do good to humanity, whenever you can. Don't be anxious for *Shaibalini*—I shall be here to watch her. But you must not meet her without my permission. If you act up to my advice, immense good could be done to *Shaibalini*".

After this, *Chandra Shekhar* took leave of his preceptor. *Ramananda Swami* then imperceptively entered into the cave, in that dismal darkness. The incidents which took place after this, are already known to our readers.

Chandra Shekhar took along with him, poor distracted *Shaibalini* to *Ramananda Swami*, in the hill-monastery, we have spoken of. He appeared before the *Swami* with *Shaibalini* and weepingly said, "Oh my venerable preceptor! what have you done—what is this?"

Ramananda Swami closely observed *Shaibalini* for a while and then said with a smile,

"It is all right—you need not be anxious in the least. Rest here with *Shaibalini* for a couple of days. After that, take her home along with you. There, keep her in the very house she used to be before—request those who were her constant companions to be with her always. Ask *Pratap* to come there every now and then. I shall come and meet you there later on."

Chandra Shekhar brought *Shaibalini* to his home, at *Bedagram*, as advised by his preceptor.

II

THE FATAL ORDER

The struggle between the *Nawab* and the English now commenced. With it, began *Mir Kashim's* fall. At the very outset, *Mir Kashim* was defeated at the battle of *Katwa*. After that, *Gurgan Khan's* treachery gradually became manifest. The hopes which the *Nawab* had centered in *Gurgan Khan*, now completely vanished away. At this critical juncture, the *Nawab* was every day losing his self-possession. He made up his mind to put to death all the English prisoners. He began to ill-treat everyone. While he was in this pitiable plight, *Makammad Taki's* letter about *Dalani* reached his hands—it added fuel to the fire. The English played false with him—his commander-in-chief was appearing to be untrustworthy—the Goddess of Fortune, presiding over his kingdom, seemed to have deserted him, and was he to believe, above and over all these, that *Dalani* too was faithless? The *Nawab* could endure no more. He wrote to *Mahammad Taki*, "You need not send *Dalani* here—put an end to her life with poison."

Mahammad Taki himself went to *Dalani* with the *Nawab's* cruel letter. *Dalani* was surprised to see *Mahammad Taki* before her. She lost her temper and said, "What is this, sir? Why are you insulting me in this way?" *Mahammad Taki* slapped his forehead in pretended grief and cunningly said, "Ah me! the *Nawab* is displeased with you."

Dalani smiled contemptuously and said, "Who brings you this news?"

"If you will not believe me," said *Mahammad Taki*, "please read the royal message".

Dalani. Then you have not been able to read it aright.

Mahammad Taki then handed over to *Dalani* the *Nawab's* letter, bearing the state seal. *Dalani* read it and threw it away; she laughed and said, "This is a forged letter. Why are you playing tricks with me? Is it because you want to die?"

Mahammad Taki. You need not be afraid of your life—I can save you.

Dalani. Oh, I see you have some motive—you have come to frighten me with a forged letter *Mahammad Taki*. Then let me tell you the real story. I wrote to the *Nawab* that you had been living in *Amyatt's* boat as his mistress; hence the fatal order.

Hearing this, *Dalani* contracted her eye-brows; her broad forehead, which was hitherto without a furrow, now shrunk into wrinkles, as if, the placid bosom of the *Ganges* was suddenly stirred up into ripples. *Mahammad Taki* was frightened at this sight. *Dalani* then asked in a dignified voice, "Why did you write so?" *Mahammad Taki* related to her everything and when he finished, *Dalani* said, "Let me see the royal message again." He again handed over to her the *Nawab's* letter. She read it through and through and examined it very closely—she was convinced that it was really the *Nawab's* message. She, therefore, asked, "Where is poison?" *Dalani's* words surprised *Mahammad Taki* beyond measure. The coward said, "What will you do with poison?"

Dalani. What is the *Nawab's* order?

Mahammad Taki. He has commanded me to put an end to your life with poison.

Dalani. Then, where is poison?

Mahammad Taki. Do you really think of taking poison?

Dalani. Why should I not obey the order of my royal master?

Mahammad Taki was put to shame. He said, "What has been has been, you shall not have to take poison. I shall devise some means to save your life."

Dalani's eyes flashed fire. She rose up and striking a dignified attitude said, "The man or woman who stoops so low as to live on the mercy of a moral wreck of your stamp, is even worse than your wicked-self—better give me poison."

Mahammad Taki gazed at *Dalani*. He found that she was a faultless creation of beauty and charmingly young. The river of her beauty was then just being filled up by the exuberant flood of youth, and her beautiful mould was about to attain its perfection, under the vivifying influence of the sweet spring of life. It seemed as if spring and autumn had combined together to produce the matchless charm, she wore about her. He thought within himself, "The beautiful lady, I am now beholding before me, is panting under grief, but how sweet and pleasant it is to feast my eyes on her beauty! Oh, my God! why have you made sorrow so charmingly beautiful? What shall I do with this distressed girl of matchless beauty—this torn flower in the bloom of fragrance— this joyous boat in the midst of the battering waves—oh, where shall I keep her?" *Satan* whispered into *Taki's* ears, "Within your own heart."

Mahammad Taki then said to *Dalani*, "Listen to my advice, fair lady, dedicate your life in love to me—you shall not have to take poison."

Hearing these rude words, *Dalani*—we feel ashamed to say—gave a kick to *Mahammad Taki*. The villain, however, did not give her poison and slowly left the room, casting askance glances at her, as he went out.

Dalani then threw herself on the floor, overpowered with grief and emotion. She wept bitterly and exclaimed, "Oh thou mighty king of kings—my life's beloved lord—my all in all, what a cruel sentence have you passed on your faithful and devoted *Dalani*! You want me to end my life with poison—why should I not, if you desire it? To me, your love is nectar and your displeasure the bitterest venom in the world—when you have been annoyed with me, I have already taken poison—is venom more tormenting than your displeasure? Oh mighty king—light of the world—God's trusted representative—incarnation of justice and mercy—my only stay in life—where are you now? I shall, in obedience to your command, take poison with joy and alacrity, but it is my only regret that you will not be before me to see it."

A maid-servant, named *Kariman*, used to attend on the *Begum*, at *Murshidabad*. *Dalani* called the maid before her. She then gave all her ornaments to the woman and said, "Secretly, *Kariman*, very secretly, get me such a medicine from the physician as I may fall asleep never to rise again. Sell these ornaments to pay the apothecary's bill—the balance, whatever it may be, you may take for yourself."

Kariman saw that *Dalani's* eyes were full of tears and she could at once understand what *Dalani* had meant. At first she refused, but *Dalani* repeatedly offered her inducements and the foolish woman, at last, agreed to carry out the order for lucre.

The apothecary gave a medicine. Forthwith, one of *Mahammad Taki's* attendants ran to his master and reported, "Just now *Kariman* has bought poison from *Hakim Mirza Habib*."

Mahammad Taki caught hold of *Kariman* immediately. She made a confession of the whole thing and said that she had already handed over the poison to *Dalani Begum*. Thereupon, *Mahammad Taki* came to *Dalani* in all haste, and he found that the *Begum* was seated on the floor, with folded hands and up-turned eyes—an incessant and unbroken stream of tears from her beautiful expanded eyes was drenching her cloth—an empty cup was lying before her—*Dalani* had taken the poison!

Mahammad Taki anxiously enquired, "What was in that cup?"

"Poison," replied *Dalani*. "I am not a traitor like you—I always take delight in obeying my master's command. It is now your duty to take what is still left in the cup and follow me."

Mahammad Taki did not say a word—he remained standing, quite motionless. Slowly and gradually *Dalani* laid herself down on the floor. She closed her eyes—everything became dark—*Dalani* left this cruel world for ever!

III

The Emperor and his Wealth

Mir Kashim's army retreated from *Katwa* after being beaten there by the English, and as hard luck would have it, they sustained another defeat at *Gheria*—the *Mahamedans* were again routed and scattered all around by the English, like dust before a strong gale. The remains of the vanquished force rallied together and took shelter at *Udyanalla*. There, the *Mahamedans* were now making trenches to check the advance of the English.

Mir Kashim appeared there in person. After his arrival there, one of his officers, *Syed Amir Hossain*, brought to the *Nawab's* notice that a prisoner was most anxiously soliciting an interview with him—that the prisoner had something very important to communicate to the *Nawab* and was quite unwilling to give it out before any other person.

Mir Kashim enquired, "Who is that person?"

"The prisoner is a woman," replied *Amir Hussain*. "She comes from Calcutta. *Mr. Warren Hastings* sent her here with a letter; in reality, she is not a prisoner. My humble-self received the letter, because it had reached me before the war broke out—if I have done wrong by doing so, I am here before your majesty to receive any punishment that your royal-self may desire to inflict on me."

After this, *Amir Hossain* read out to the *Nawab* the letter, he had received from *Warren Hastings*. It ran as follows:—

"I do not know who this woman is; she appeared before me in a piteous condition and begged to be sent to the *Nawab*, as she was quite helpless in *Calcutta* and had no other means to have recourse to. War, it seems, will soon break out between you and ourselves, but the people of our race have no quarrel with women and I, therefore, send her to you. I know nothing beyond what I have already said."

After hearing the letter, the *Nawab* ordered the woman to be brought before him. *Syed Amir Hossain* went out and after a while returned with the woman. The *Nawab* saw that she was no other than *Kulsam* herself. He was violently annoyed and asked,

"What do you want, wretched slave—death?"

BANKIM CHANDRA CHATTERJEE

Kulsam looked the *Nawab* in the face and for a time remained staring at him. She then said in a stern voice, "*Nawab*! Where is your *Begum*—where is *Dalani Biby* gone?"

The fearless manner in which *Kulsam* addressed herself to the *Nawab* surprised and, to some extent, frightened *Amir Hossain*—he made a profound bow to the *Nawab* and retired from the place. *Mir Kashim* then said,

"You will be soon sent to the place where that wicked soul now rests."

Sterner than before, *Kulsam* replied, "Yes, I shall be, but you too shall have to follow her—it is for this reason why I have come to you. On my way here, I heard that *Dalani Begum* had committed suicide—tell me, is it true?"

"Suicide"! replied the *Nawab* in astonishment. "She was doomed to death by royal orders. You were her accomplice in all her crimes—I will see that you are torn off into pieces by dogs—"

Kulsam could bear no more—she threw herself down on the floor and burst into a wail. She then began to scold and abuse the *Nawab* in no measured language. Hearing her, the guards, the officers of the state and the *Nawab's* personal attendants, came there in all haste—one of them ran towards *Kulsam* and, but for the *Nawab*, would have lifted her up by the hair; the *Nawab* was taken aback and so, he forbade the man to molest her. *Kulsam* then said,

"It is good that you all have come here—I will now unfold to you a thrilling story. The *Nawab* will immediately order my death—no body will come to know of the story, if I do not relate it to you before my death; so, you all listen to me. There is a foolish ruler of *Bengal* and *Behar*, named *Mir Kashim*. He had a *Begum* whose name was *Dalani*—she was the sister of the *Nawab's* commander-in-chief, *Gurgan Khan*."

Hearing this, no one again meddled with *Kulsam*—all who were present there, began to look at each other's face, in surprise—a feeling of curiosity was roused in them. The *Nawab* too remained silent—*Kulsam*, in continuing her story, said,

"*Gurgan Khan* and *Daulatunnesa* left together *Ispahan* and came to *Bengal* to earn their livelihood. When *Dalani* entered *Mir Kashim's* palace, as a slave girl, both the brother and the sister promised to help each other up."

After this, *Kulsam* related to them, in detail, what happened on the night, she and *Dalani Begum* had called at the commander-in-chief's place. She had heard from *Dalani* all about the conversation the *Begum* had with

Gurgan Khan, on that fatal night and so, could tell her hearers all about it; she also related how the *Begum* had been prevented by the commander-in-chief from re-entering the castle—how the strange hermit had come to their help—how they had got shelter in *Pratap's* house—how *Dalani* had been carried away from there by the English, who had mistaken her for *Shaibalini* and lastly, how after *Amyatt's* death, *Dalani* had been cast on the isolated bank of the *Ganges* by wicked *Foster*. She then said,

"There is no doubt that *Satan* had come upon me, at that moment, or why should I leave the *Begum* alone? The pains and sufferings of that wicked Englishman had moved me, and I—but let that go; it was my belief that the *Nawab's* boat was coming after us and that the *Begum* will be taken on it, or why should I leave her alone there? But, I have been sufficiently punished for my folly. To speak the truth, immediately after the *Begum* had left us, I entreated and implored *Foster* to also drop me down—but he did not do so. On my arrival at *Calcutta*, I asked every man I came across with, there, to send me back here, but nobody took pity on me. Later on, I came to know that *Warren Hastings* is always kind to the needy and the distressed—I went to him and fell at his feet, with the prayer, that I might be sent back here. It is through his kindness that I have come here and you can now put an end to my life—I have no desire to live in this world any more."

So saying, *Kulsam* began to weep.

On that immensely rich and gorgeous throne, bedecked with jewels, casting on all sides their lustre in innumerable beams and rays, was seated the *Nawab* of *Bengal*, with down-cast eyes. The sceptre of his vast kingdom was about to slip out of his hand—it could not be retained in spite of all possible endeavours, but where was now that unconquerable kingdom, which would have remained his without any effort whatsoever?

The *Nawab* had taken care of the thorn instead of the rose—*Kulsam* had truly said—"The ruler of *Bengal* is a fool."

The *Nawab* then said to the noblemen of his court, "Listen to me, it is beyond my power to retain this kingdom any more. The slave girl has truly said, that the ruler of *Bengal* is a fool. If you can save this kingdom from ruin, good and well—I shall take leave of you all and quit this place; I shall either take shelter within the female quarters in the castle at *Ruhidas*, or lead the life of a mendicant."

The *Nawab* paused for a while—his strong and majestic body began to shake with emotion—he controlled his tears with much effort and again said, "Listen to me, my faithful friends! if the English kill me, like *Seerajuddaulah*, do not fail to bury me by the side of the grave of my dear and devoted *Dalani*—remember this is my last request to you. I cannot speak any more—you may now leave me alone; but before you go away, do something for me—I like to see that *Taki Khan* once. *Ali Ibrahim Khan*! I have no better friend than yourself, in this world—it is my request to you, that you should anyhow bring before me that treacherous *Mahammad Taki*." *Ibrahim Khan* saluted the *Nawab* and coming out of the Durbar-tent, mounted on his horse and rode away.

The *Nawab* then said, "Is there any one else, who is willing to help me?"

All present, folded their hands out of reverence and stood before the *Nawab* to receive orders.

The *Nawab* said,

"Can any one of you bring *Foster* before me?"

"I will forthwith start for *Calcutta* to find out *Foster*," said *Amir Hossain* respectfully.

The *Nawab* paused for a while and then said,

"As for *Shaibalini*? Can any one manage to bring her here?"

"She must have returned to *Bedagram* by this time," submitted *Mahammad Irfan*, with folded hands. "I will go and bring her here."

After this the *Nawab* said,

"Can any one find out the hermit, who gave shelter to *Dalani Begum* at *Murshidabad*?"

"If you desire, I can go to *Monghyr* for the hermit after I have found out *Shaibalini*," replied *Mahammad Irfan* with a respectful bow.

The *Nawab* then inquired, "How far is *Gurgan Khan* now?"

One of the councillors said, "It is reported that he is marching towards *Udayanalla* with his main force—but he has not yet arrived here."

The *Nawab* thereupon muttered,

"Force! Force! whose force is it?"

"It is his, after all", whispered some one.

The councillors now took leave of the *Nawab*. Just as they left, the *Nawab* rose from his brilliant throne of gold, threw away from his head the crown with its glittering diamonds, tore off the beautiful necklace of pearls, and cast aside all other valuables from his person; he then threw himself down on the floor and cried out, "Oh, my beloved *Dalani*! where are you now?"

Such is the worthlessness of regal pomp, in this world.

IV

John Stalkart

It has been said in the preceding chapter that *Kulsam* had an interview with *Mr. Warren Hastings*. In relating to him, in detail, the incidents which brought her to *Calcutta*, she told him all about *Foster's* misdeeds. In history, *Warren Hastings* appears to be a great oppressor of men. But, it is an undeniable fact that men of action often become oppressive for the sake of their duty. The man upon whose shoulder rests the enormous responsibility of defending an Empire, is often compelled, on Imperial considerations, to play the role of an oppressor, although personally, he may be kind and even righteous. Those who are builders or defenders of an Empire, consider it expedient to oppress particular individuals when it is calculated to benefit the whole Empire. In fact, those who are competent, like *Warren Hastings*, to establish kingdoms and empires cannot possibly be unkind or unrighteous. The man who has not the heart to feel for others and has not the courage to adhere to the rigid principles of morality, can, by no means, perform a great task like that of founding an Empire; for, his mind is not broad—it is narrow—and it has not been, and will never be, the privilege of narrow-minded men to accomplish great deeds.

Warren Hastings was both kind and righteous. At the time we are speaking of, he was not the Governor. After sending *Kulsam* to the *Nawab*, he set himself to find out *Foster*. He found that *Foster* was ill. He, therefore, first of all, made arrangements for his treatment. Under the care of a good physician, *Foster* soon recovered. After that, *Warren Hastings* started an enquiry to ascertain *Foster's* crimes. *Foster* was frightened and he made a confession of his guilt. Thereupon, *Warren Hastings* moved the Council and had *Foster* dismissed from the Company's service. It was his desire to drag *Foster* before a court of justice, but as it was not possible to get the witnesses and as *Foster* had already suffered much from the consequences of his sinful conduct, *Warren Hastings* desisted from it.

Foster could not appreciate the step which *Warren Hastings* had taken—he was extremely selfish and narrow-minded. He thought within himself that the punishment was too severe for his crime. Like a mean and ungrateful guilty servant, he became angry upon his old masters and resolved to do them harm, with all the zeal of an enemy.

At that time, one *Dyce Schembre*, a Swiss or a German by nationality, was serving *Mir Kashim*, as one of the leading officers in the army. This man was popularly known as "*Samaru*". *Samaru* was now present at *Udayanalla*, with the force under his command. *Foster* came there to meet him. He, first of all, very cleverly managed to send a messenger to *Samaru*. The latter thought that much information about the plans of the English could be obtained if *Foster* were taken into his army. So, *Foster* was admitted into *Samaru's* camp, where he cunningly assumed the name of *John Stalkart*. *Lawrence Foster* was in *Samaru's* camp when *Amir Hossain* was about to set out in search of that wicked profligate.

After leaving *Kulsam* in the proper place, *Amir Hossain* set himself to find out *Foster*. At the very outset, he came to know from his attendants that an Englishman had enlisted himself as a soldier in the *Nawab's* army, and that he was now in *Samaru's* tent. *Amir Hossain* went there to see the man.

Samaru and *Foster* were engaged in a conversation when *Amir Hossain* entered into the tent. After he took his seat there, *Samaru* introduced to him *Foster*, as *Mr. John Stalkart*. *Amir Hossain* then began a talk with *Stalkart*. In course of his conversation he asked,

"Do you know *Mr. Lawrence Foster*?"

Foster's face became red with fear—with downcast eyes, he faltered out,

"*Lawrence Foster*? No—I don't remember."

"Have you ever heard his name?" asked *Amir Hossain*.

Foster remained silent for a time and then said,

"His name—*Lawrence Foster*!—yes—let me see—no, I have never heard."

Amir Hossain did not go any further—he introduced other topics; but, he could see that *Stalkart* was not speaking freely. More than once, he rose up to go, but *Amir Hossain* entreated and made him sit again. He could feel that the Englishman knew everything about *Foster*, but would not give out anything.

A while after, *Foster*, all on a sudden, put on his hat and remained seated, as before. *Amir Hossain* knew that this was against the English etiquette. Besides, when *Foster* was putting on the hat, *Amir Hossain's* eyes accidentally fell upon a scar on *Stalkart's* head. Did *Stalkart* put on his hat to hide that mark? *Amir Hossain* took leave of *Samaru* and left his tent. He then went to his own quarters and calling up *Kulsam* before him, asked her to follow him. *Kulsam* did so, and *Amir Hossan* led her to the entrance of *Samaru's* tent. Leaving her there, he entered into the tent and said to *Samaru*,

"If you will permit, one of my slave girls will appear before you and pay her respects—she is coming here in the interest of an important business."

Samaru gave permission. *Foster's* heart began to beat violently—he rose up to go, but *Amir Hossain* smiled and taking *Foster's* hand in his, made him sit again. *Kulsam* was brought in and she was surprised to see *Foster* there—she stood staring at him, quite motionless.

Amir Hossain asked her,

"Who is this Englishman?"

"Lawrence Foster," replied *Kulsam*.

Forthwith, *Amir Hossain* caught hold of *Foster's* hand.

"What have I done?" asked *Foster* in pretended innocence.

Amir Hossain did not give any reply and said to *Samaru*,

"Sir, I have the *Nawab's* order to arrest this man. Please order a sepoy to take him, under arrest, along with me."

Samaru was surprised beyond measure and he asked,

"What is the matter?"

"I will tell you everything afterwards," replied *Amir Hossain*.

Samaru ordered a sepoy and he took away *Foster* in chains.

BANKIM CHANDRA CHATTERJEE

V

To Bedagram Again

Chandra Shekhar brought *Shaibalini* to *Bedagram*, with great difficulty. He again entered into his once-abandoned home after a long, long time. He saw that his house had become more hideous than wilderness itself. There was almost no straw on the roofs of his thatched houses—most of it had been carried away by storms; the roofs of some houses had come down and the straw on them, had been eaten up by cattle—all the bamboos of those fallen houses had been taken away by the neighbours, to be used as fuel. The courtyard had overgrown with weeds—reptiles of every description were found to crawl about most freely within it. The doors and windows of the houses had been stolen away by thieves. All the rooms were found open—not a single article was found within them—some had been taken away by burglars and some had been removed by *Sundari*, to be carefully preserved in her own house. The rains had free access into the rooms and had made them quite damp with moisture—the house was full of filth and dirt. Rats, bats and cockroaches were found to parade within the house, in gangs. After many long and weary days, *Chandra Shekhar* again entered into that house with *Shaibalini* and cast a deep sigh. He looked around and noticed the spot where he had burnt into ashes his valuable treasure of old books. He then called out,

"*Shaibalini!*"

Shaibalini did not make any reply; she sat at the entrance of the house and was gazing at the stalwart *Karabi*, as if, it resembled a phantom, which she had seen, in a dream, in by-gone days. She did not say a word in reply to *Chandra Shekhar's* numerous questions—she was looking about, with her eyes unusually expanded and with a meaningless smile on her lips—she once laughed aloud and pointed out something with her finger.

In the meanwhile, the news spread in the neighbourhood, that *Chandra Shekhar* had returned with *Shaibalini*. Many were coming to see them—*Sundari* came first of all.

Sundari did not know that *Shaibalini* had gone mad. She first of all, made obeisance to *Chandra Shekhar*, whose garb of an ascetic surprised her. She then looked at *Shaibalini* and said to *Chandra Shekhar*,

"After all, you have done well in bringing her back—everything will be all right, if she would undergo a penance."

But *Sundari* was astonished to see that, unlike *Hindu* women, *Shaibalini* neither moved away nor drew her veil, and began to laugh at *Sundari*, although her husband, *Chandra Shekhar*, was there. *Sundari* thought that it was a fashion which *Shaibalini* must have learnt from her English companions. So thinking, she went up and took her seat by *Shaibalini*—but she took every care that even her cloth may not come in contact with that of *Shaibalini*; for, she had lost her caste. She then said with a smile,

"Look here, can you recognise me?"

"Yes, I can," replied *Shaibalini*. "You are *Parbati*."

"What a pity!" exclaimed *Sundari*. "You have forgotten me so soon?"

"Why should I forget you, dear?" said *Shaibalini* vacantly. "Don't you remember I beat you black and blue, when you spoiled my dinner by touching my dishes? *Parbati*—my sweet sister! just sing a song.

> *My heart's cherished secret is that,*
> *Where is the maid on gallant's lap?*
> *Where is the moon within clouds' wrap?*
> *Vain, oh vain, is my covert-craft!*

You see, *Parbati*, I am miserably confused—I feel, as if, some one is absent—he was here, but now he is not—some one is expected, but he does not turn up—I have come somewhere, but I feel I have not—I want some one, but I know him not."

Sundari was taken aback and she looked *Chandra Shekhar* in the face, anxious to know what the matter was. *Chandra Shekhar* called her near him. He then whispered into her ears that *Shaibalini* had gone mad. *Sundari* now understood everything. She remained absolutely silent for a time. First of all, her eyes looked a bit brighter with moisture— they then became wet, and finally, tears came out of them in torrents— *Sundari* began to weep. Blessed are women in this world! This *Sundari*, on another occasion, had sincerely wished for *Shaibalini's* death—she had prayed that *Shaibalini's* boat might sink with her; but now, none felt more than *Sundari* for *Shaibalini*.

After a while, *Sundari* wiped away her tears and again took her seat by *Shaibalini*. Slowly and gradually she drew *Shaibalini* into a conversation—slowly and gradually she began to remind her of the things of the past—but poor *Shaibalini* could not recollect anything. *Shaibalini* had not lost her memory altogether, or how could she recollect the name of *Parbati*? But her brain was so deranged, that everything got confused within her. She remembered *Sundari*, but she could not recognise her.

First of all, *Sundari* sent *Chandra Shekhar* to her own place, for a bath and breakfast. She then set herself to make that almost dilapidated house fit for *Shaibalini's* habitation—one by one, all her neighbours came to assist her; necessary articles were forthcoming from all sides.

On the other hand, *Pratap* returned home from *Monghyr*, after he had stationed his armed men at the right places. On his return there, he heard that *Chandra Shekhar* had come back—he, therefore, immediately left for *Bedagram* to meet him.

On that very day, a little before *Pratap's* arrival, *Ramananda Swami* appeared there. *Sundari* heard with great pleasure that *Chandra Shekhar* would administer medicine to *Shaibalini* according to the great *Swami's* instructions. An auspicious hour was fixed for the purpose.

VI

Spiritual or Psychic Force

We cannot say what the drug was, but *Chandra Shekhar* came to administer it after self-ablution and rigid observance of such other rites as lead to the purification of the soul. He was naturally a master of his passions and propensities and had greater control over hunger and thirst than ordinary men. But to meet the demands of the present occasion, he had rigorously abstained from any food, and during the last few days had kept himself absolutely engaged in the contemplation of God—he had not allowed any other thought to creep into his mind.

At the appointed hour, *Chandra Shekhar* began to arrange the preliminaries to the administration of the sacred drug. He asked the maid-servant, whom *Sundari* had engaged for *Shaibalini*, to get ready a bed, which she did. *Chandra Shekhar* then asked *Sundari* to make *Shaibalini* lie down on it. *Sundari* had to apply force; for, *Shaibalini* could not be made to do anything easily. She would not touch *Shaibalini*, as she had lost her caste; but, *Sundari* did so on the present occasion, only because she would undergo self-ablution, as usual, on her return home from *Shaibalini's* place.

Chandra Shekhar now said to those who were present in the room, "You all go out—come in when I ask."

When all went out, *Chandra Shekhar* placed the cup, containing the drug, on the floor. He then asked *Shaibalini* to sit up. She did not do so—she began to sing lowly. He fixed his eyes upon her firmly, and began to give her handfuls of that drug, at short intervals. *Ramananda Swami* had told him that the medicine was nothing else but the holy water from his sacred *Kamandalu*. He had also told him, on being asked, that it would give *Shaibalini* spiritual powers.

After this, *Chandra Shekhar* began to mesmerize *Shaibalini*. Slowly and gradually her eyes were closed and she was soon over-powered with mesmeric sleep.

Chandra Shekhar now called out, "*Shaibalini!*"

"My lord," responded she, in her sleep.

Chandra Shekhar. Can you say who am I?

Shaibalini. Yes, you are my husband.

Chandra Shekhar. Who are you?

Shaibalini. I am *Shaibalini.*

Chandra Shekhar. What place is this?

Shaibalini. Bedagram—your home.

Chandra Shekhar. Can you say who are waiting outside?

Shaibalini. Pratap, Sundari, and a few others.

Chandra Shekhar. Will you tell me why did you leave *Bedagram*?

Shaibalini. Because, *Foster* had taken me away.

Chandra Shekhar. Why couldn't you recollect all these things so long?

Shaibalini. I remembered them, but I could not rightly express myself.

Chandra Shekhar. Why?

Shaibalini. On account of my insanity.

Chandra Shekhar. Is it real or pretended?

Shaibalini. It is absolutely real.

Chandra Shekhar. But, now?

Shaibalini. It is a dream—I have got back my senses through you.

Chandra Shekhar. Then, will you speak the truth?

Shaibalini. Yes, I will.

Chandra Shekhar. Why did you go with *Foster*?

Shaibalini. For *Pratap.*

Chandra Shekhar was startled—the things of the past appeared before him in the vividness of reality. He asked,

"Is *Pratap* your paramour??

Shaibalini. Fie!

Chandra Shekhar. Then what is he to you?

Shaibalini. We were two flowers blooming in the same garden and on the same stalk—why did you tear us asunder?

Chandra Shekhar breathed a deep sigh. He was a man of unlimited wisdom and he could understand everything. After a while, he asked,

"Do you remember that you swam along with *Pratap* in the *Ganges*, on the night, *Pratap* made his escape from the boat of the English?"

Shaibalini. Yes, I do.

Chandra Shekhar. What talk had you with him that night?

Shaibalini briefly related everything. Hearing her, *Chandra Shekhar* thanked *Pratap* at heart. He then asked,

"Why did you live with *Foster*?"

Shaibalini. I lived with him in name only. It was my hope that I would meet *Pratap*, if I would go to *Purandarpur* with *Foster*.

Chandra Shekhar. In name only! Are you then still chaste?

Shaibalini. I am not, only because I had dedicated my life to *Pratap*—I am a great sinner.

Chandra Shekhar. Otherwise?

Shaibalini. Otherwise I am perfectly stainless.

Chandra Shekhar. In respect of *Foster*?

Shaibalini. In respect of *Foster*, I am absolutely innocent.

At this stage, *Chandra Shekhar* cast upon *Shaibalini* sharp and penetrating glances and carried on the mesmeric operations, more vigourously. He urged,

"Tell me the truth."

Shaibalini, although unconscious in her mysterious stupor, contracted her eye-brows and said,

"I have told you the truth and nothing but the truth."

Chandra Shekhar again breathed a deep sigh and said,

"Why then did you, for nothing, suffer yourself to lose the *Brahmanic* caste, by living with an alien infidel?"

Shaibalini. You are well-versed in all the scriptures of divine authority and I appeal to your judgment to say, whether I have really lost my caste or not. I have never taken any food at *Foster's* hand—never drank from the pot he might have touched; I cooked my food, with my own hands, every day—a *Hindu* maid-servant used to serve me. I had, no doubt, to live with *Foster* in the same boat, but that was on the sacred waters of the holy *Ganges*.

Chandra Shekhar remained silent, with downcast eyes—he reflected for a long time and then said within himself, "Alas! how cruelly have I treated *Shaibalini*—I was about to make myself responsible for the death of an innocent life!"

After a while he asked *Shaibalini*,

"Why didn't you say all these things before?"

Shaibalini. Who would believe me?

Chandra Shekhar. Who can testify to what you say?

Shaibalini. *Foster* and *Parbaty*.

Chandra Shekhar. Where is *Parbaty* now?

Shaibalini. She has died at *Monghyr* about a month ago.

Chandra Shekhar. Where is *Foster*?

Shaibalini. He is now in the *Nawab's* camp, at *Udayanalla*.

Chandra Shekhar remained absorbed in meditation for a time and then inquired,

"Can you say whether you will be cured of the malady you are now suffering from?"

Shaibalini. You have given me your spiritual strength and with its help, I can very well perceive that through your grace and the efficacy of your sacred drug, I shall soon recover.

Chandra Shekhar. Where do you desire to go after your recovery?

Shaibalini. If I get poison I shall take it, but I fear the hell.

Chandra Shekhar. Why do you like to put an end to your life?

Shaibalini. What place have I to resort to, in this world?

Chandra Shekhar. Why, my house?

Shaibalini. Will you take me back?

Chandra Shekhar. If I do?

Shaibalini. In that case, I shall devote my heart and soul to your service; but then, it will bring stain on your good name.

Just as she concluded, the tramp of a horse was heard at a distance. Thereupon *Chandra Shekhar* said,

"I have no spiritual force within me—you have got *Ramananda Swami's* divine strength and with its help, tell me what noise is that.

Shaibalini. It is the foot-tramp of a horse.

Chandra Shekhar. Who is coming on it?

Shaibalini. Mahammad Irfan—one of the *Nawab's* military officers.

Chandra Shekhar. Why is he coming?

Shaibalini. To take me to *Udayanalla* along with him—the *Nawab* wants to see me.

Chandra Shekhar. Did he send for you on *Foster's* arrival or before it?

Shaibalini. No, he ordered at the same time to bring both of us before him.

Chandra Shekhar. No cause for anxiety—you better sleep in peace.

Chandra Shekhar called in every one, and said to them, "*Shaibalini* is now sleeping. When she will wake up, give her the draught in that pot. Now, one of the *Nawab's* officers is coming here to take her away with him to the *Nawab's* camp, tomorrow. You all should go with her."

"Every one was surprised and frightened to hear this. They all asked, "Why should she be taken before the *Nawab*?"

"You shall come to know every thing presently," replied *Chandra Shekhar* briefly. "There is absolutely no cause for anxiety."

On *Mahammad Irfan's* arrival there, *Pratap* engaged himself in his reception. On the other hand, *Chandra Shekhar* secretly related to *Ramananda Swami* all what *Shaibalini* had said in her hypnotic sleep. Hearing him, the *Swami* said, "Both of us must be present at the *Nawab's Durbar*, tomorrow."

VII

In the Durbar

The last ruler of Bengal was seated on his Imperial throne, in a large tent, at *Udayanalla*, to receive audience. *Last* because, those who became *Nawabs* after *Mir Kashim* were rulers in name only.

The *Nawab* in his regal robe, studded with pearls and diamonds, sat majestically on his high throne of gold, bedecked with jewels of every colour and description, with the superb state crown on his head, shining with its precious brilliants. On his two sides, stood, with folded hands, his numerous attendants, in well-formed rows—the high officials, with the permission of their royal master, were seated on a carpet, in a kneeling attitude, silent and motionless. The *Nawab* asked,

"Are the prisoners all present?"

"Yes, if it please your majesty," replied *Mahammad Irfan*, with a bow.

The *Nawab* expressed his desire to see *Lawrence Foster* first. *Foster* was accordingly brought in and made to stand before the *Nawab*. He asked *Foster*, "Who are you?"

Lawrence Foster could feel that there was now no escape for him. He thought within himself, "So long I have only brought disgrace to my race and nationality—today I will die like an Englishman." He said to the *Nawab*,

"My name is *Lawrence Foster*."

Nawab. To what nationality do you belong?

Foster. I am an Englishman.

Nawab. Then you are my enemy—why did you come to my camp?

Foster. I have no explanation to give—I am now in your hands and you can inflict on me any punishment you like. You need not ask me why I came here—if you do so, you will have no answer from me.

The *Nawab* instead of being angry, laughed aloud and said,

"Well, I see you are fearless. Will you tell me the truth?"

Foster. Englishmen never tell lies.

Nawab. Is it? All right, we will see that now. Who was telling me that *Chandra Shekhar* is here? Get him before me if he is come.

Mahammad Irfan brought *Chandra Shekhar* before the *Nawab*. The *Nawab*, pointing his finger at *Chandra Shekhar*, asked *Foster*,

"Do you know him?"

Foster. I have heard his name but I do not know him.

Nawab. All right. Where is *Kulsam*?

Kulsam was brought there and the *Nawab* asked *Foster*,

"Do you know this woman?"

Foster. Yes, I do.

Nawab. Who is she?

Foster. She is one of your maid-servants.

Nawab. One of you go and bring *Mahammad Taki* here.

Mahammad Irfan accordingly brought in *Taki Khan* in chains. The treacherous wretch was hitherto wavering as to which side he would take in the struggle between the *Nawab* and the English; so, he was not able to go over to the enemy's side. Besides, the commanders of the *Nawab's* forces, knowing him to be faithless, used to keep him under vigilant watch. It was, therefore, quite easy for *Ali Ibrahim Khan* to bring him to *Udayanalla*, as a prisoner.

The *Nawab* did not even look at *Taki Khan*. He simply said to *Kulsam*, "You now relate in detail, how you went to *Calcutta* from *Monghyr*."

Kulsam related the whole story, as clearly as she could. She gave out all that she knew about *Dalani Begum*. She then folded up her hands, and with tears in her eyes, addressed herself to the *Nawab* as follows:—

"My lord! I have a complaint to lodge, at this your royal court, against that cruel murderer, *Mahammad Taki*—pray listen to me. That faithless and treacherous man has duped my royal master by making certain false and libellous allegations against his queenly wife. The wretched sinner has, without the least hesitation or pain, destroyed the life of *Dalani Begum*, that jewel of a woman, as if, that precious thing was as insignificant a trifle as a poor ant. My lord! justice, therefore, demands that this great sinner should be crushed like an ant."

"It is a lie," faltered out *Mahammad Taki*. "Who are your witnesses?"

Kulsam's eyes were dilated with emotional grief and she roared out,

"Who will bear testimony to what I say? Look up—God is my witness! Place your hand on your heart—you are my witness. If any other person's deposition is necessary, ask that Englishman and he will say whether my story is true or not."

Thereupon, the *Nawab* asked *Foster*,

"What do you say—is the maid-servant's story true? You had been with *Amyatt*, and you have just now said that Englishmen do not tell lies."

Foster gave out what he actually knew about *Dalani Begum*. His statement convinced every one, present there, that *Dalani* was absolutely stainless. *Mahammad Taki* remained silent, with down-cast eyes.

Chandra Shekhar then stepped forward and thus addressed himself to the *Nawab*,

"My lord, I can also testify to what the maid-servant has said. I am that very hermit, who came to your *Begum's* help, on the isolated bank of the *Ganges*."

Kulsam immediately recognised him and said,

"Yes, it is he, indeed!"

Chandra Shekhar now said to the *Nawab*,

"My lord, if this Englishman is truthful, pray, ask him one or two more questions."

The *Nawab* understood what *Chandra Shekhar* had meant and said,

"You better put the questions—the interpreter will explain them to *Foster*."

Chandra Shekhar then asked,

"You said a little before that you have heard the name of *Chandra Shekhar*—he is no other than myself. Why did you take away—"

"Please stop," interposed *Foster*, "you need not bother yourself with any question. I am free, as I do not fear death—it depends entirely upon my sweet will whether I shall give any answer to your questions or not; I am determined not to say anything in reply to any of your queries."

"Then bring *Shaibalini* here," ordered the *Nawab* to his men.

Shaibalini was accordingly brought in. At first, *Foster* could not recognise her—she was now lean and emaciated—she had put on a dirty and ragged *Shari*—her locks were flowing about in a wild manner and had lost their glossy lustre, through utter neglect—there was the smile of madness in her lips, and the vacant looks of insanity in her once-intelligent eyes! *Foster* shuddered at this sight.

The *Nawab* asked him, "Do you know her?"

Foster. Yes, I do.

Nawab. Who is she?

Foster. She is *Shaibalini*—*Chandra Shekhar's* wife.

Nawab. How do you come to know her?

Foster. You better inflict on me any punishment you like—I will not give any answer to this question.

Nawab. It is my desire to see you torn into pieces by hounds.

Foster grew pale—his limbs began to tremble with fear. He got over his nervousness a little after and said,

"If it is your desire to put an end to my life, pray, order any other form of capital punishment."

Nawab. No. Tradition has it, that in by-gone days the practice among the rulers was to bury alive a culprit, sentenced to capital punishment, up to the waist, and then let loose at him trained dogs to tear him limb by limb. After each attack of the fearful hounds, salt used to be showered upon the wounds of the unfortunate victim. The dogs would go away when they had satisfied their hunger with the culprit's flesh, and the man would be left in that miserable plight, half-dead, to be finished by them when they felt hungry again. I order such a punishment for you and the treacherous *Taki Khan*.

At this, *Mahammad Taki* burst forth into a hideous cry of distress, like an afflicted brute. *Foster* knelt down and with folded hands and up-turned eyes, began to pray to God for his deliverance—he said within himself, "Oh, omnipotent Father! I have never in my life taken your holy name or thought of your divine grace. I have all along sinned against you. It never occurred to me that you are omnipresent. But I venture to invoke your help, because I am helpless today—oh, thou friend of the needy and the succour of the distressed! come to my help and save me from the impending danger."

Good readers! don't be surprised at this. Even the man who does not believe in the existence of God, invoke his divine help in the hour of gloom—he invokes it with all the sincerity and devotion of his heart. *Foster* too prayed, and devotedly prayed, for Heaven's mercy.

While lowering his eyes after prayer, *Foster* quite unexpectedly saw, at the entrance of the tent, a striking, hoary-headed personality, casting acute and penetrating glances at him. The wonderful man wore a loose scarlet; he had long matted hair and a flowing grey beard—he had sacred symbols painted all over his body with the ashes from his sacred altar of sacrificial fire. *Foster* could not take away his eyes from that imposing spectacle and as if charmed, fixed them upon those of the strange figure, before him. Gradually his mind was absolutely overpowered by the influence of that vision. A little after, his eyes became heavy with sleep and a peculiar hypnotic influence benumbed his limbs. It seemed to *Foster* that the lips of the wonderful man, before him, were moving, as if, he was speaking something. Gradually, a voice of thunder reached his ears—he heard some one saying,

"I will save you from the threatened punishment. You better answer to what I ask—are you *Shaibalini's* paramour?"

Foster gazed at the poor distracted *Shaibalini* and said,

"No, I am not."

Every one present there distinctly heard *Foster* saying, "No, I am not." That mysterious voice, resembling a roaring thunder, was again heard. *Foster* could not make out whether it emanated from the *Nawab* or *Chandra Shekhar* or some one else—he simply heard a solemn voice asking,

"Why was then *Shaibalini* kept in your boat?"

Foster cried out,

"My mind was completely captivated by the fascinating charms of *Shaibalini's* beauty and I was led to snatch her away from her home. I kept her in my boat in the belief that she might be attached to me; but, I soon found that I had been acting under a delusion—she was verily my enemy. When I met her in my boat for the first time, she brought out from her waist a sharp knife and said to me in a threatening attitude, 'If you will come within my cabin, this knife will end your and my life—look upon me as your mother.' I could therefore never go within her cabin—I did not even touch her."

Every one heard this. *Chandra Shekhar* then asked,

"How could you then make her eat your food, knowing that it will lead to her excommunication from the society?"

"She did not take, even for a day, my food or anything that I might have touched," said *Foster* in an earnest and impressive tone. "She used to cook her food with her own hands."

Question. What she used to take?

Foster. She used to take only rice with milk.

Question. What about the water she used to drink?

Foster. She would invariably get it herself from the *Ganges*.

Boom! Boom! Boom!

"What is that?" inquired the *Nawab* in surprise. "Alas, it is the cannon's roar," replied *Mahammad Irfan*, in a mournful voice. "The *English* have attacked our camp."

Forthwith, people within the *Nawab's* tent began to rush out, in wild disorder. The firing grew heavier and oftener and the roaring cannons were heard nearer and nearer, as if, they were approaching by leaps and bounds—the blood exciting note of battle was struck by the military bands, and the air all around was filled with war's rattle. The noise of the hoofs of galloping steeds, the metallic jingle of the combatants' arms and armours and the shouts and war-cries of the fighting soldiers, all mixed together, and resembled the hustle and commotion of a boisterous sea— the sky was enveloped with sulphurous smoke. So unexpected was this outburst of warlike fury, that it seemed, as if, during the dead of night, when the whole universe is lulled to sleep by the fostering care of nature, the angry ocean, swollen with rage, rushed forward and encircled the camp, quite unawares.

All on a sudden, the officers and the attendants of the *Nawab* rushed out of the tent, in all haste—some to go to the field of battle and some to make ignominious escape. *Kulsam, Shaibalini, Chandra Shekhar* and *Foster* also came out; only the *Nawab* and the captive, *Taki Khan*, remained within the tent.

After a while, the enemy's shells began to fall on the *Nawab's* tent. Thereupon, the *Nawab* rose up and unsheathing his sword, thrusted it, with his own hand, into the heart of his treacherous prisoner. *Taki Khan* fell on the ground dead, and the *Nawab* walked out of the tent.

VIII

IN THE FIELD OF BATTLE

C handra Shekhar came out of the tent with *Shaibalini* and found *Ramananda Swami* standing at the entrance. The *Swami* said to *Chandra Shekhar*, "Well, what will you do now?"

"How am I to save *Shaibalini*? enquired *Chandra Shekhar* anxiously. "Bullets and balls are coming from all sides like hails—nothing can be seen through smoke—where to go?"

"There is no cause for anxiety," replied *Ramananda Swami*, in an assuring tone. "Don't you mark the direction the *Mahamedans* are running to? What prospects can there be for the *Nawab* when his soldiers are taking to heels at the very outset of the battle? It seems to me, that the English are exceptionally lucky, strong, courageous and skilful—a day will, perhaps, come when they will bring under their subjection the whole of the sacred *Hindusthan*. Let us better follow the routed *Mahamedans*. I do not care much about you or myself, but we cannot but be anxious for *Shaibalini*."

They now followed the beaten soldiers of the *Nawab*. After proceeding a little, they suddenly saw before them a band of well-armed *Hindu* fighters, in imposing uniform, coming out of a narrow pass to meet the English, with soldier-like courage and enthusiasm. In the centre of the column was the leader, mounted on a superb battle-steed. All the three recognised that it was none else but *Pratap* himself. *Chandra Shekhar* became uneasy at the very sight of *Pratap*. Advancing he said,

"*Pratap*! what brings you to this fatal field of battle? Better go back."

"I was coming in search of you," replied *Pratap*. "Come, I will conduct you to a safe place."

He then placed *Ramananda Swami, Chandra Shekhar and Shaibalini* within his small army, and proceeded with them towards the direction he came from. All the passes and accessible ways in that hilly tract were well-known to *Pratap* and he was, therefore, able to take them far away from the battle-field, very soon. While they were thus proceeding, *Pratap* heard from *Chandra Shekhar* all about what happened in the *Durbar*. After relating to him the whole story, *Chandra Shekhar* said,

"*Pratap*! you are really beyond any praise—you know more of this world than I do."

Pratap was surprised and looked *Chandra Shekhar* in the face. *Chandra Shekhar* then said in a voice almost choked with emotion,

"Now I have come to know, beyond the shadow of a doubt, that *Shaibalini* is perfectly stainless. I shall take her into the bosom of my family again, and if for this I have to undergo a penance for the satisfaction of our society, I shall ungrudgingly do it. But, I cannot be happy—fate has ordained it otherwise."

"Why?" enquired *Pratap* anxiously. "Has not the *Swami's* medicine proved efficacious?"

"Not yet," replied *Chandra Shekhar*.

Pratap was much pained—tears came into his eyes. *Shaibalini* could see this from within her veil. She moved away a little and beckoned *Pratap* to come near her. *Pratap* alighted from his horse and came to *Shaibalini*. She then said to him, in a voice inaudible to others,

"Will you allow me to tell you something in whispers? I will not say anything objectionable."

Pratap was taken by surprise. He said,

"How is it, did you then feign insanity?"

Shaibalini. Yes, now it will look like that—since I left my bed this morning, I have been feeling quite myself. Did I really become mad?

Pratap's countenance flashed with joy. *Shaibalini* could perceive his feelings and she at once whispered into his ears, in an eager manner,

"Keep quiet, don't say anything now. I myself will tell every thing—I only await your permission."

Pratap. Why should you at all need my permission?

Shaibalini. If my husband takes me back, will it be proper for me to participate in his love and affection without making a confession of my sins, before him?

Pratap. What do you want to do?

Shaibalini. I want to tell him every thing regarding my past and crave his forgiveness.

Pratap thought for a while and then said,

"All right, you may tell him every thing. I wish and pray that you may be happy this time."

Pratap was carried away by emotion and he shed tears.

"It is impossible for me to be happy," said *Shaibalini* in a melancholy but serious tone. "So long as you shall be in this world, I shall not be happy—"

"Why, *Shaibalini*?" enquired *Pratap* in surprise.

"So long as you shall be in this world, pray, do not appear before me," replied *Shaibalini* with emotion. "The mind of a woman is extremely frail and I do not know how long I shall be able to keep it under my control. We must not meet again, in this life."

Pratap didn't make any reply. He quickly mounted his horse and set off for the battle-field. His little band of warriors followed him.

When *Chandra Shekhar* saw *Pratap* going, he asked,

"Where are you going?"

"To the field of battle," was *Pratap's* brief reply.

"Don't—for God's sake, don't go—there is no escaping out of the hands of the English," cried out *Chandra Shekhar* anxiously.

"*Foster* is still alive—I am going to put an end to his sinful life," replied *Pratap* in an impressive tone.

Chandra Shekhar ran up to *Pratap*, as fast as he could, and caught hold of the reins of his horse. He then said,

"Why should you kill *Foster*, dear *Pratap*? The wicked shall be punished by God. Are we the dispenser of justice? It is only the narrow-minded who take revenge on their enemies—good souls always forgive."

Pratap was surprised—his heart overflowed with joy. He had never before heard such a noble utterance from any man. He alighted from his horse and made obeisance to *Chandra Shekhar. Pratap* then said,

"In this selfish world, there are few praiseworthy men like your nobleself. I will do *Foster* no harm."

Pratap again mounted his horse and rode off towards the battle-field. Thereupon, *Chandra Shekhar* again cried out,

"*Pratap*, why are you, then, going to the battle-field?"

Pratap turned back his face and said, with an exceedingly sweet and pleasant smile,

"I have some business."

He, then, spurred his horse and galloped away.

Pratap's smile made *Ramananda Swami* extremely anxious and uneasy. He said to *Chandra Shekhar*,

"You go home with *Shaibalini*. I shall go to perform an ablutionary rite in the sacred waters of the holy *Ganges*. I shall come back and meet you in a couple of days."

Chandra Shekhar said, "I am awfully anxious for *Pratap*."

"I will bring you news about him," replied *Ramananda Swami*.

The *Swami* then gave *Chandra Shekhar* and *Shaibalini* leave to go and himself proceeded towards the battle-field. In that bloody field, enveloped with an endless volume of smoke and filled with the heart-rending groans of the dying and wounded, *Ramananda Swami* began to move about, in search of *Pratap*. Here and there, he saw hundreds of human bodies, lying in heaps—some without life, some almost lifeless and others profusely bleeding from torn limbs and wounded breasts; some crying out, in a most piteous manner, for a drop of water to quench their unbearable thirst and others calling their father and mother, brothers and sisters, friends and other dear ones, in agony of despair. *Ramananda Swami* searched for *Pratap* among them, but did not find him. He next saw a large number of horsemen, their body besmeared with blood, galloping away on their wounded steeds for their very life, crushing under their feet the unfortunate wounded lying disabled on the battle-field. The *Swami* looked for *Pratap* among those routed warriors, but did not find him. He then came across with a large band of infantry-soldiers, bathed in blood, running away at a breathless speed, in terror of a fearful enemy. He watched them minutely, as they passed away, in the hope of finding *Pratap* among them, but all in vain. He then sat down under the shade of a large tree, fatigued and exhausted. Close to that spot, a sepoy was running away in all haste to save his life. *Ramananda Swami* said to him,

"I see, every one of you is taking to heels—who is it, then, that fought the battle?"

"No one except a *Hindu*, who has shown great courage and heroism," replied the soldier briefly.

" . . . I bless you, and wish you a speedy recovery"

"Where is he now?" enquired *Ramananda Swami*, rather anxiously.

"Look for him near the fort," answered the sepoy in hot haste and ran away. *Ramananda Swami* went there. He found that the struggle was over and in one place, some English and Hindu soldiers were lying in a heap. *Ramananda Swami* began to search for *Pratap* among them. One of the *Hindus* groaned out in bitter agony. *Ramananda Swami* dragged him out and found that it was *Pratap*—mortally wounded—still alive, but on the point of death. *Ramananda Swami* fetched some water from the nearest place and gave *Pratap* a drink. *Pratap* recognised him and made an effort to raise himself to make obeisance to the *Swami*, but could not pick up strength to do so.

"You need not make any effort," said the *Swami*, in an affectionate tone. "All the same, I bless you and wish you a speedy recovery."

"Recovery! It is near at hand," said *Pratap* with great difficulty, quite conscious of his end. "Now, pray for my soul."

"Why did you come to this fierce battle, in spite of our warning," asked *Ramananda Swami*, in a mournful voice. "Did you do so for *Shaibalini's* sake?"

"Why should you think so, please," calmly interrogated *Pratap*.

The *Swami* said,

"When you were talking with *Shaibalini*, it seemed to me from her movements, that she was no longer insane and that she has not forgotten you altogether."

"*Shaibalini* asked me not to meet her again," observed *Pratap* touchingly. "I could feel that so long as I would live in this world, *Shaibalini* or *Chandra Shekhar* could not possibly be happy. I thought it was quite improper for me to live as a thorn in the way of those who are my best well-wishers and objects of love and veneration. It is for this reason, why, in spite of your dissuasion, I came to this bloody field of battle to sacrifice my life. I am taking leave of this world; for, if I live, one day or other, *Shaibalini* may lose her constancy and go astray again."

Tears came into *Ramananda Swami's* eyes—no one had seen tears in his eyes before. He said with emotion,

"*Pratap*! in this world, you alone know how to live for others—we are humanitarians in name only. In your next life, you will be entitled to the eternal bliss of heaven."

After a brief pause, *Ramananda Swami* continued, "Listen to me, dear *Pratap*! I have been able to read through your mind—even the conquest of the whole universe cannot be favourably compared with your glorious triumph over your passions—you used to love *Shaibalini*, most dearly."

Ramananda Swami's last words went straight into *Pratap's* heart. They infused a new spirit into his inert and almost lifeless body and he roared out, as if, a lion had been roused from sleep,

"What will you understand, you are an ascetic! What man is there in this world who can fathom the love I bear to *Shaibalini*? Who will appreciate with what devotion and constancy I have loved *Shaibalini* during these long sixteen years? I am not attached to her with any evil motive—my love is nothing but a desire to sacrifice my life for the sake of the object of my love. Throughout day and night, this feeling has been flowing through my veins with every particle of my blood—no man has yet, or could ever, come to know of it—why have you raised this question at the time of my death? I felt that this love will not be blissful in my present life and so I am leaving this body. My mind has, perhaps, been stained and who can say what change may not come upon *Shaibalini's* life, if I do not disappear from this world, for ever? I felt that nothing but my death could secure pleasure and happiness for *Shaibalini* and *Chandra Shekhar*, and so I made up my mind to take leave of you all. You have come to know of my secrets—you are wise and intimately familiar with all the scriptures of divine authority—you now tell me what will be an adequate penance for my sins. Do I stand guilty before God? If so, will the sacrifice of my life redeem my faults?"

"This is more than what I can say," replied *Ramananda Swami* sorrowfully. "It is not within the scope of human knowledge to answer your question in a definite manner; even the scriptures cannot help the solution of such a problem. None but the Almighty Ruler of the realm, you are going to, can say what the futurity has in store for you. But, this much I can say that if there is any reward prescribed in the economy of Providence for those who become masters of their passions and propensities, then you are sure to enjoy for ever the eternal joy and bliss of heaven. If the religious merits of a man are to be judged by the efficiency of the control he is capable of exercising over his mind and body, I can unhesitatingly say that even the celestial beings are not as virtuous as you are. If the unselfish dedication of one's life to the service of his fellow beings can at all entitle him to a place in the holy realm of heaven, your claim on such a reward is greater than even that of the great *Dadhichi*. I pray to God, with all the sincerity of my heart and the devotion of my soul, to so ordain that I may be, in my next life, as powerful a ruler of my senses and sensibilities as you are."

Ramananda Swami became silent. Slowly and gradually the last vital spark of life was out and *Pratap* left this world for ever.

The stately figure of a stainless soul now lay cold and stiff on a bed of grass.

Then, farewell *Pratap*, farewell to thee! Blithe spirit! go to that eternal land of glory, where it is not difficult for one to free himself from the fetters of flesh and blood—where there is nothing like blind fascination in respect of beauty and where love is not profane, as we find in this shabby world of ours. Go to that etherial region, where beauty, love, or happiness knows no end or decay and where happiness leads to eternal virtue. God-speed to thee, in thy journey to that great unknown and mysterious land, where every living soul is conscious of the sorrows of each of his fellow beings—where every one safeguards the virtues of another, delights to sing in the praise of others and where no one ever feels the necessity of sacrificing his life for the sake of a fellow creature—go, noble spirit, go to that glorious land of eternal peace and contentment! If, there, at your feet, you get myriads of *Shaibalini*, you would not care to love them!

THE END

A Note About the Author

Bankim Chandra Chatterjee (1838–1894) was an Indian novelist, poet, and journalist. Born into a Bengali Brahmin family, he was highly educated from a young age, graduating from Presidency College, Kolkata with an Arts degree in 1858. He later became one of the first graduates of the University of Calcutta before obtaining a Law degree in 1869. Throughout his academic career, he published numerous poems and stories in weekly newspapers and other publications. His first novel, *Rajmohan's Wife* (1864), is his only work in English. Between 1863 and 1891, he worked for the government of Jessore, eventually reaching the positions of Deputy Magistrate and Deputy Collector. *Anandamath* (1828), a novel based on the Sannyasi Rebellion against British forces, served as powerful inspiration for the emerging Indian nationalist movement. Chatterjee is also known as the author of Vande Mataram, a Bengali and Sanskrit poem set to music by Bengali polymath and Nobel laureate Rabindranath Tagore.

A Note from the Publisher

Spanning many genres, from non-fiction essays to literature classics to children's books and lyric poetry, Mint Edition books showcase the master works of our time in a modern new package. The text is freshly typeset, is clean and easy to read, and features a new note about the author in each volume. Many books also include exclusive new introductory material. Every book boasts a striking new cover, which makes it as appropriate for collecting as it is for gift giving. Mint Edition books are only printed when a reader orders them, so natural resources are not wasted. We're proud that our books are never manufactured in excess and exist only in the exact quantity they need to be read and enjoyed.

Discover more of your favorite classics with Bookfinity™.

- Track your reading with custom book lists.
- Get great book recommendations for your personalized Reader Type.
- Add reviews for your favorite books.
- AND MUCH MORE!

Visit **bookfinity.com** and take the fun Reader Type quiz to get started.

Enjoy our classic and modern companion pairings!

Printed in the USA
CPSIA information can be obtained
at www.ICGtesting.com
JSHW022344140824
68134JS00019B/1685